# BIG
# F@!KING
# DEAL

## LAWRENCE ALLAN

1st edition

First published in 2023 Copyright © 2023 Lawrence Allan All rights reserved.

ISBN: 979-8-9861761-3-0 (ebook)

ISBN: 979-8-9861761-2-3 (paperback)

Designed by Yummy Book Covers

**Other Books by Lawrence Allan**

Big Fat F@!k-up

For more information about Lawrence Allan,

check out **LawrenceAllanWrites.com**

or subscribe to his newsletter at

**LawrenceAllanWrites.substack.com**

*For everyone that had to live up*
*to their reputations...*

# Big F@!king Deal

# 1

THE BIG, DUMB jerk standing at my office door grinned like he had won a million bucks. A formerly athletic man who had gone soft, his shoulders had become thicker, his waistline rounder, and he had stuffed himself into what he probably thought was his best suit, not even bothering with a tie. His face was pink from a recent shave and his brown hair had gone gray.

"Jimmy!" he shouted at me, like he hadn't walked out on his family.

"Dad?" I managed.

Paul Cooper took that as an invitation and lumbered in, opening his arms wide as if this was actually a happy family reunion.

Spoilers: It wasn't.

Paul Cooper, a failed actor and family man, had left my mother — and, by extension, my younger sister and me — about fifteen years ago without much of an explanation. Or maybe he had given one. At the time I was sliding deep into my addictions, with my career cratering... Or maybe because my career was cratering, I got deeper into my addictions? Tomato, potato. Anyway, maybe Paul *did* explain himself back then, but I wasn't exactly paying attention to things like that. And with Mom running her law firm and my sister, Erika, the rock of the Cooper family, keeping the house together, maybe no one else had time to catch me up.

And now, here he was, Paul Cooper in the flesh, embracing me as I choked on his cheap cologne. Good times.

I looked behind him at Nora, my twenty-something assistant, who blushed with embarrassment. She could read the room and had realized that it had been a mistake for her to leave Paul unattended in reception to come and tell me he was here. Nora, simply the best in every other situation, had the decency to look apologetic as she looped a bit of blonde hair behind her ear.

This Monday morning had been going so well too. Saturday I had solved the biggest, most public case of my life as a private detective. It had been a case no one (see also: my mother) thought I would be able to solve. After all, I was a former child star and recovering addict who had become the in-house detective of his mom's law firm. As such, I had just been thrust back into the limelight. That's not exactly a winning pitch. No one was *really* expecting much from me.

In the end, I saved the client, helped put Cooper and Associates back on firmer financial ground, and was back in the public's good graces after years of being a Hollywood cautionary tale. This Nickelodeon Kids Choice Award winner was back on top.

Instead of celebrating, however, I had a whole new problem to deal with.

"Should I call security?" mouthed Nora, carefully enunciating each word.

I considered it for a hot second — how good would it be to see him dragged away? — but, no. I shook my head. This was something I should take care of. Quietly. No good would come of my mother and/or sister finding him here.

The embrace ended, but before I could step away, Paul grabbed me by the shoulders, still grinning. He was always happy to pretend that no moment was actually uncomfortable. "You're looking great!" He lightly bro-punched me in the arm. All vim and vigor with this guy.

"Yeah. Well. Sobriety. It'll do that." And that's all I really had to give him. What do you say to someone you haven't seen or heard from in forever — especially if it's your father and you've already come to terms with the fact that *(a)* he was an asshole and *(b)* you totally don't have *any* daddy issues? Ok, *maybe* no daddy issues.

Hating the silence, Paul spun away from me and looked out my office windows. "Wow. What a view."

It totally was. From Cooper and Associates' offices in Century City, you could see the rest of L.A., all the way to the Pacific.

Paul nodded at the horizon, then turned back around and offered a hand to Nora. "Paul Cooper." He nodded in my direction. "His dad." As if that was somehow going to impress her.

I pulled his hand away lest she be tempted to shake it. I didn't need Paul forming any relationships with the people in my life. He wasn't going to be here for long. "This is Nora. My assistant."

"Jimmy, I'm trying to say hello," he said with a smile.

"Yeah, yeah, I get that." I did not need Paul Cooper committing sexual harassment in front of me. "Does anyone else know you're here?"

He frowned, pulling his head back. "Anyone else? Like who?"

JFC. "Like Erika. Or *Mom*. This is her law firm, after all."

He grinned again and said proudly, "Oh, no. I was trying to surprise you all."

Paul Cooper had a talent for asking for forgiveness rather than permission.

Oh, shit. Did I get that from him?

Saving that particular existential crisis for another day, I turned and I asked Nora, "Do you think either of them saw him?"

She shook her head. "Both are in meetings. At least, I know your mother is. I haven't seen your sister."

A quick nod and I said, "Perfect. Go swear reception to secrecy — make sure they know their lives depend on it — and then clear a path from my office to the elevators."

Nora turned and left.

Paul snorted. "Come on, Jimmy. What are you doing? This isn't funny."

"Isn't *funny*?" I peeked out of my office door, making sure Mom wasn't marching down the hall with a torch and pitchfork.

She wasn't. Instead, Greta Cooper was behind the glass walls that made up the conference room, sitting at the head of the table, holding court in an emerald-green suit. Her gray hair was combed back, her fingers laced together on the table. Lucky for me, she seemed deep into the process of castigating one of the associates.

"It's *hysterical*," I assured him, not letting my eyes waver from my mother. The woman had the reaction time of a coiled viper. "A laugh riot, Paul."

He put his hands on his hips, all bluster. "Oh, I'm *Paul* to you now?"

I glared at him. "Better than Deadbeat Dad."

He blushed.

I had wounded him. Good.

I closed my office door and turned on him. "What are you even doing here?" I realized I had asked the wrong first question. I revised it. "Where the fuck have you *been*?"

He hesitated. "Vegas."

"Vegas? Four-hours-*away* Vegas?"

Paul Cooper shrugged. "Is there another one?"

I squeezed my forehead, hoping to keep my brain from exploding. "You've been so close the whole time, and you never thought of calling or — "

"I'm here now!"

Unbelievable.

There was a gentle double knock on the door. I opened it to find Nora standing there. "It's clear," she whispered with a thumbs-up. Then she headed back to reception.

I said to Paul, "We're leaving now."

"Where are we going?"

"*You're* going back to Vegas."

He put his arms out wide, pleading. "I just got here!"

I grabbed him by one of his outstretched arms and yanked him into the hallway. "And it's been great," I muttered. "Five stars. I'll be talking about the whole five minutes to my therapist for weeks."

I should really think about getting a therapist.

He leaned back like a toddler, trying to slow us down. I

grunted as we passed Dave, the office manager who now sat at my old desk, eating one of the donuts I had brought in as celebratory treat for everyone. He paused, donut to mouth, and watched the struggle go by.

"Can't we at least talk?" said Paul as he huffed and puffed in protest.

"What have we been doing this whole time?" I countered.

He tried out his Dad voice. "*James.*"

It failed to impress. Too little, too late.

We entered reception. Nora pushed the elevator button, rapid-fire, while the two receptionists found something to do to keep their eyes busy.

"At least let me buy you breakfast," he offered.

"It's eleven in the morning."

"Lunch then!"

"Still eleven in the morning, Paul."

He sighed, defeated.

The elevator appeared with a ding, and Nora stopped pushing the button. The door opened, and I nudged Paul inside. I stepped in after — I couldn't trust he'd get into his car by himself — and jabbed the lobby button. I nodded my thanks to Nora as the door closed.

As we headed down, Paul harrumphed in the corner of the elevator, crossing his arms. "This isn't how I thought it would go."

"Really? Sorry to disappoint. But as I learned early, life is populated by people who will disappoint you." I shook my head. "I gotta ask…" Did I? I did. "After all this time, why are you here now?"

Of course, it wasn't just now that he was here, Paul had also stumbled onto *my* day. *My* moment.

Paul was about to reply when the elevator paused halfway down. The doors opened, and a couple of lawyers in flashy suits stepped on, staring at their phones. The whole building was riddled with them.

Paul tried to catch my eye, wanting to answer my question, but I changed my mind, instead taking a real interest in the elevator's stainless steel ceiling. I didn't need the lawyers listening in on my family drama.

The doors finally opened onto the lobby. The lawyers got out, and Paul and I followed.

"We could get coffee," he said.

I guided him to the exit. "I don't want to get coffee with you."

"Fifteen minutes. That's all I need."

"Fifteen minutes feels like a big ask."

I pushed through the revolving doors, and we were outside. It was already hot and bright, and I regretted leaving my sunglasses upstairs. That meant I'd have to squint and squinting makes my weird faces weirder.

(I don't *actually* have a weird face. My face is fine. But you can only read so many discussions in the tabloids and online about your face and the faces it makes before you get self-conscious about the whole thing. The lesson here, kids: Never read the comments.)

Paul pulled out his shades and slipped them on. Of course, he had *his*.

"Listen, Jimmy — "

I held out my hand. "Your ticket."

"My what?"

"Your valet ticket. I assume you parked here."

He reached into his pocket, then paused. "Oh, shit. We left before someone could validate my parking."

This guy.

"The first twenty minutes are free."

He pulled out the ticket and handed it over. I snatched the ticket from him and went to the red-vested valet, who looked at my father and then me. "Yes. He's my dad. Can you just...?"

The valet shrugged, took the ticket, grabbed the keys from the rack, and jogged down into the garage to get the car.

Paul wandered over, hands in his pockets. "Quite a place."

I rolled my eyes. "Mom's had her firm here for, like, twenty years. You've *been* here."

He looked back up, at the building and then around. "Yeah. OK. Yeah, I have. But" — he pointed around — "the area has changed a lot. It didn't look familiar."

And he was telling the truth.

I have this thing. I can sense when someone's lying to me. Maybe it's all that time I spent as an actor. I can see how a person holds themselves, hear the tone of their voice. If they lie, I get a sort of buzz in the back of my head, which is pretty helpful in my line of work.

And, oddly, the whole time I had been around Paul, no buzz had been detected.

"I really want to get some coffee. You want some coffee?" It wasn't quite a smile, but his lip curled, and for a second there, I saw my dad again. The guy who had been my partner in crime. The guy with a big heart who could encourage and entertain. The guy who had been there for me.

Until he wasn't.

"I'm good," I said.

He tried again. "I just want to catch up."

Buzz. He didn't.

"Just google me. You can find all the highlight reels."

A dull gray Prius arrived. The valet stepped out and handed the keys to my dad. Reluctantly, he took them. As he gripped them in his hand, he said, "I just need a few minutes. To talk about some opportunities."

I shook my head no.

Paul nodded and took a step toward his car.

"Dad?"

He and I both turned.

*Shit.*

Erika stood there, cup of coffee in hand, green eyes staring wide at Paul Cooper. She had my brown hair, though she had had the good sense during puberty to grow a few inches taller. She got her fashion sense from our mom, and today was dressed in an elegant dark blue suit.

I wanted to disappear. I had been so close to getting away with it. But then Erika just *had* to go out for coffee, totally ignoring the fact that there's perfectly terrible coffee available in our break room.

Erika finally managed to get out, "What are you doing here?"

Sensing an opportunity to throw a Hail Mary, Paul turned to his daughter. "I was hoping to talk to Jimmy about — "

I stepped in and said, "Leaving. He was leaving."

"*Jimmy,*" Erika snapped. She turned to him. "Seriously, what are you doing here? What do you want to talk to Jimmy about?"

A flicker passed over Paul's face. Maybe he was going to be forthcoming. But, no. "You know, this and that." He shrugged. "Maybe I should've called before dropping in." He smiled at Erika. "You look great. Maybe we could do dinner? This week?"

I could see the hundred different things that Erika wanted to say. It was just a question of which one would be said first.

Paul didn't give her a chance. He slipped into his car, stiffing the valet on his tip, and was gone.

Which left me holding the bag.

"What just happened?" my sister asked, incredulous. Her green eyes narrowed. "Were you trying to sneak him out?"

Busted.

She sucked her teeth. "Unbelievable. Did he say what he wanted?"

"He didn't."

"He wants to talk to you about *something*."

"Well, I don't know what it is."

She slugged me in the shoulder.

"Ow! What was that for?"

"You deserved it." She pointed after the departing Prius. "Why didn't you ask him?"

"Because I don't really want to know."

She grunted, studying her coffee cup. "Did Mom see him?" she asked.

"No."

"Because she would have a stroke if she knew he just showed up." Erika shook her head at the entire situation. "Find out what he wants, Jimmy. And, like, fix it. Make everything go back to how it was." And with that, she headed back inside, leaving me alone.

I took her meaning, but if I was being honest, I wasn't sure if I wanted everything to go back to *normal* normal. I had really been enjoying the new normal, except for the last ten minutes.

# 2
—

"YOU'RE A BIG fucking deal, Jimmy Cooper," said the movie producer, looking up from his coffee table, where he was using his production company's credit card to arrange cocaine into nice, snortable lines.

I should've left at that point. In my experience, once the coke comes out, parties always take a turn for the worst.

The producer had called my office to invite me to a party on Saturday night at his Hollywood Hills home — on the L.A.-facing side no less. Who in their right mind would turn *that* down? Hours before the party, my anticipation turned up to eleven. Who I was going to run into? What great food would I eat? Sure, attending the party had meant cancelling plans I had made with a certain amazing, very attractive

LAPD Robbery-Homicide detective I had met on my last case, but... she would totally understand.

If I had actually told her about the party.

OK, fine. There was the distinct possibility I was avoiding a potential relationship with Detective Violet Ito that I would ultimately just blow up. I liked her — a lot — and I didn't want to do that.

It had been almost a week since I had seen or heard from Dad, and just like I hadn't told Ito my whereabouts, I also had *not* done what Erika had asked me to do. I hadn't reached out, I hadn't found out what he wanted to talk to me about because, quite frankly, I was enjoying this new normal. I was back on top.

The producer, Eric, was in his late forties and dressed like he was in his twenties. He wore a tight, black T-shirt and cargo shorts with sandals. With his wrinkle-free face and blonde hair, it kind of worked. We were hanging out in the game room next to the patio, where the party was raging. He put the credit card aside and pointed to the coke, offering me some.

I shook my head no. I was on the wagon and planned on staying that way. That's not to say I didn't have a good time on coke. I did. It's the reason why drugs are so hard to quit. You're always looking to feel that amazing again. Diminishing returns being what they are, though, hopefully you hit rock bottom before they kill you from all the fun you're supposed to be having.

So Eric snorted as I looked away at anything else and took a drink of my club soda. My eyes landed on his collection of eighties horror movie posters. When I looked back, he was making a face I recognized. The coke was dripping down the back of his throat from his nasal passageway. That took me back. Ugh. *Why* was I here?

Eric swallowed and pointed up toward a hidden speaker near the ceiling. "Love this fucking song." It was "Today" by The Smashing Pumpkins. He nodded his head. "It's going to open the movie."

I raised an eyebrow. "Which movie?"

His head jiggled. "The *movie*." He grunted, a little bothered he had to explain. "We're making a movie about The Smashing Pumpkins. Going to call it *Smash*. Maybe. Could be *Smashed*; that sounds more active. Don't know. Doesn't matter. We'll decide when we make the poster." He leaned back, getting comfy on the leather couch. "We're using the band as a way to look at that whole nineties grunge thing. This shit comes back around, you know?" He rubbed his nose. "It's going to be classy. Like *awards* classy. It's going to totally elevate me. I'm gonna be like an A-*plus* lister." He grinned, satisfied with his play on words.

"Sure."

The smile faded. "We just got to get Billy to sign off on us using the music."

"Billy? As in Billy Corgan, the lead singer?" I relaxed a little, captivated now. Eric being on a first-name basis with Billy Corgan got my attention.

Eric nodded. "The guy's a real genius, but he's also a real dick. He doesn't want anything to do with the movie. Which is bullshit."

"Because it'll be classy." Disappointed once the reality of the non-relationship was revealed to me, I went back to wondering why I was here.

He cocked his head, trying to work out whether or not I was making fun of him. I worried he had entered the paranoid phase of his coke habit.

Eric decided I wasn't making fun of *him*. He laughed. "*You* get me." More laughter. He scrubbed his nose, and wiped his hand on his cargo shorts, and did another line. He pointed at me. "It's awesome you're here." He nodded, agreeing with himself. "I want you to know, I want to be in the Jimmy Cooper business."

"You want to be a private detective?" I said, confused. "And give up all this fame and fortune?"

He scoffed, fanned his hand across the room. "I'm a *movie* producer, Jimmy. Why would I give that up?"

That was a fair point.

"No, I want to be in business *together*." He bumped his fists. "I want to make a movie with you, dummy!"

Blood drained from my face. Dammit. You don't just

get invited to a party in the Hollywood Hills when you've been out of the business as long as I have. There's always something. And it's generally a buck to be made.

"I'm not an actor anymore," I protested.

His laugh sounded like a machine gun. "*You're* not going to be in the movie. It'll be based on your story. Something real. People eat the real shit up all the time." He tapped the coffee table for emphasis. "You put 'based on actual events' in a trailer or before a movie, people will go crazy. *Fargo* says it's based on real events, and that's a fucking *lie*." He leaned forward and snorted the last rail of coke. "I bet you got some great stories. I put you in a room with a writer, and we'll come up with something great."

"Something classy."

He smirked. "Not too classy, am I right?" He laughed again, but it slowed to a stop when he saw the look of bewilderment on my face. "You do know what this is about, right?" He pointed around the room. "I thought you knew why you were here."

I shrugged, nervous as I waited for the other shoe to drop.

"Your father " — there it was, the other shoe — "he said you would totally be into pitching me some ideas." He paused. "Are you into it?" He paused. "It doesn't seem like you're into it." He pushed himself off the couch and put an arm around my shoulder. "But don't say no right away."

I could barely hear him. When did he talk to my father?

Why did he talk to my father?

"Have a drink, have a bite," he said, ushering me to the game room's door and out into the party.

I floated outside as I wondered how did he and my father even connect. How did this *happen*?

"Meet a girl, make some bad choices." Eric smiled. "We'll meet up. Lunch or something. I'll call your agent."

Hah, joke's on him. My agent stopped returning my calls years ago.

Eric turned away and greeted another guest. She was a redhead in her twenties, wearing a tight, white T-shirt that ended above her belly button and slick, black latex leggings. She handed him a drink and leaned into him, laughing. I don't even think he had said something funny, but I was pretty sure it didn't matter.

Spinning out, I headed over to the spread, near the kidney shaped pool. I wasn't going to pass up an opportunity to stuff my feelings with free food. After putting more than a healthy amount of salmon rolls on my plate, I found a chair by the pool to plop my ass in and watch the show while I stewed.

The cast of characters hadn't changed at these parties, just the faces, playing out the same old tragicomedy. There were the actors trying to outshine each other. The musicians who were too cool for school, just here for the booze. There were the directors pitching their movies to wannabe producers. And then there were the hangers-on, happy to be there, enjoying their proximity to stardom, enjoying the ability to gloat at brunch tomorrow, telling everyone what they had missed.

I was being unfair. I was angry. I thought I had been invited because... well, because I was a big fucking deal. That's what everyone was saying. And maybe I was, but my dad — I mean, *Paul Cooper* — was out there making phone calls.

"Jimmy! How are you, man?"

A guy in his late twenties stood before me in a suit jacket and T-shirt. He was lean with a bit of muscle in his chest, and had short, black hair that was just beginning to recede. In his hand was an overpriced aluminum bottle of sparkling water.

He looked vaguely familiar, and he knew me. Did I know him? That was the problem with having been famous. For whatever reason, people are on a first-name basis with you.

Shit. Did he just Billy Corgan me? Claiming a relationship where there wasn't one?

"Hey," I replied. "I'm good." I smiled, hoping that would be the end of it and I could go back to my sushi-fueled, unbridled anger at my father.

"Weird running into you here."

I couldn't begin to guess why it was weird. "Yeah." To cover the fact I had no idea who this stranger was, being agreeable seemed like the best idea.

"It's like fate."

"Sure, yeah. Fate."

Oh, God. Was he a writer? Was he going to ask me to *read* his script?

He toasted; I toasted in return. I could feel sweat running down my back. He looked *so* familiar. A name. He had a name, and it was there, on the edge of my memory. My stomach knotted up. I knew him. This wasn't a creepy interaction with a fan. This was someone I should know, and it *was* weird running into him. I kept my smile on and plowed ahead with my embarrassment.

"You've always been a big inspiration to my career," the guy said.

"Oh, OK. Great. Good to hear."

"And you did it again."

I wondered and worried what it was that I had done.

He took a breath, then admitted, "I've been kicking around for so long, looking for something new to do with my life. I didn't want to do a podcast or a vlog or whatever. Like, I'm still vital."

"Vital, yeah," I said, stuffing a piece of sushi into my dumb mouth.

"When my show ended when I turned seventeen — "

*Right.* Relief flooded over me. *He's a former child actor.* This answer, of course, prompted the next puzzle: Which *one*?

"I didn't even realize my career was over for, like, five years." He pointed at my plate. "Can I have one? They're all out at the table."

I wanted to slap his hand away, but I said, "Sure." I carefully watched as he took his *one* piece. I could only imagine where this guy — what the hell was his *name*? — was going with his story.

As he chewed, he said, "So, yeah. I'm going to become a private detective. Pretty cool, huh?"

I had no idea how to respond to this guy. *He* was going to be a private detective? *I* was the private detective.

"I always wanted to help people, so I thought about becoming a cop. But I got a history with — "

"Drugs?"

"Yeah."

Matty Goodman! *That* was his name. The weight of the world lifted off me. Matty had been a cable TV star on a sitcom aimed squarely at the kids. It had a dumb name, *The Teenage Life of Riley*, where he played Riley, who got up to hijinks. Matty had been a huge deal at the time and had a squeaky-clean image, too, so it was quite the scandal when, *shockingly,* he turned out not to be anything like his character. Like the rest of us child actors, he was a flawed human being trying to cope with the impossible pressures of stardom. His show had been on for six seasons when he got busted on a possession charge, so the powers that be decided to end it quietly and move on to the next tween idol.

"You're doing *what*, Matty?" Now that I remembered his name, I was going to use it.

He carried on. "I'm working on getting my PI license." He paused. "My agent thinks it's a great idea."

So he still had an agent. And something in his voice told me he didn't agree. "Your agent *wants* you to become a private investigator?" That didn't sound right. Not at all.

Matty took a breath. "He wants to pitch it as a reality series."

*That* sounded like an agent.

Matty's eyes followed a couple of actresses as they made their way past us, heading to the open bar. Matty smiled at them, but they didn't stop to take much notice.

"But," he continued, "I don't want to make a dumb reality show. Like, I think detective work is something I'm meant to do. The life I'm supposed to be leading." He paused. "I think I'd be really good at it. And... fulfilled." He shrugged. "Any advice?"

I looked Matty over more carefully. I realized, in his suit and T-shirt, he had styled himself after one of my press photos from the last case. I wondered if my success had become Matty's plan for success. Why reinvent the wheel when you could just copy what the other guy had done?

That's Hollywood, man.

"Advice?" I said. "Become a lawyer or a nurse or something. You'll help a lot more people."

What was I doing? I was being a real asshole.

His head tilted. "I don't want to be a lawyer or a nurse. I want to be a private eye."

"Well, it's tough work."

Matty crossed his arms, frowning. "What are you trying to say?"

What *was* I trying to say? And why was I being so mean?

I stood up. "I'm trying to say, don't do this. You'd be dealing with terrible people. It's not fun. It's not glamourous."

A fully clothed rock star jumped into the pool holding a bottle of Jack Daniels. He was soon joined by three girls in bikinis.

I waved a hand in front of his distracted face. "*Ignore* what's happening around us, OK? I'm just trying to give you the advice you were asking for. This job isn't a reality show. It isn't something you just pick up. It's quite often life-and-death."

*That* wasn't true. My work was a lot of sitting around in my car. And more often than not, it was affairs and fraud. Cut and dry.

Matty aimed a finger at me. "You're a fucking asshole, Jimmy Cooper."

Why was I being an asshole? And — just great — because

Matty had raised his voice as only an actor can, all these people were starting to notice.

"I'm trying to do something with my life," he continued. "Make myself a better person. Other people can become private detectives, too, you know."

I held firm to my plate of sushi. "Other people *are* private detectives, Matty. I'm just saying... it's weird that you, a former child star, *also* want to become a private detective. Like me. A former child star. You're pushing inspiration too far. Do I care that you're following exactly in my footsteps? Yeah, I do. It feels derivative. And everyone's going to know it. But hey, you do you, Matty."

Annnnnd scene. As everyone stared, already forming their hot takes for their social media of choice, I walked away from the party.

# 3
—

I STOOD OUTSIDE the producer's house, holding the plate of sushi I swiped when I stormed out of the party, waiting for the valet to bring my car around. I'd been a big fucking jerk to Matty — a *public* jerk, no less — and I didn't know why. It could've been the reappearance of Paul Cooper and his meddling ways. I had been rattled to find out my invite to this party was all a setup. To what end, I didn't know yet, and for the first time, I regretted not following Erika's orders to find out exactly what our father wanted from me.

I looked back at the house. Maybe it was all the ambition on display that bothered me. Everyone there was doing their best to become big fucking deals themselves. The fame and fortune Hollywood can give you is as powerful as gravity.

It's no joke about the kid coming out here with nothing and making it big.

If you make it, after all the sacrifices and hard work, it's worth it.

Unless it almost kills you.

Then you have to reevaluate.

The thing was, it had been a week since my last big case, and there wasn't anything like it on the horizon. And, as anyone in this town can tell you, you're only successful as your last hit. Emails and phone calls had been flowing in, and Nora was doing her best to field them all. But nothing was quite "right." Not for a follow up. I didn't need to be finding someone's lost dog. Or confirming that, yeah, a douchebag husband is cheating on his wife and she should leave him now.

And then here came Matty, a younger, handsomer, taller version of me, ready to swoop in and snag some clients with his effortless charm.

Was this imposter syndrome?

I turned to go back in and apologize to him. He didn't deserve to be blasted with my shit. But then my car showed up, and I thought it was best to avoid any sort of emotionally revealing moment. It wasn't a Cooper thing anyway.

I tipped the valet heavily — they are the heroes of L.A. — and hoped that Matty enjoyed the rest of his night as I headed down out of the Hills.

I turned onto Laurel Canyon Boulevard. Kindness's cover of the Replacement's "Swingin' Party" hummed out of my speakers, and I grabbed a piece of sushi from the plate on the passenger seat.

Being in this particular headspace sucked. I remembered the downsides to fame. The jealously, mostly, with that toxic bit of ambition. Maybe life didn't have to be better? Maybe life was OK just as it was. Misery comes from wanting more.

A right turn put me onto a busy Sunset Boulevard. Saturday night was one of my favorite times to see the Strip. It was showtime — all lit up; expensive cars crossing through intersections, pulling up to curbs; groups of people in front of bars and clubs in their Saturday night best; friends grabbing food, taking selfies. Adventure awaited each and every one of them. Maybe they'd get into trouble and laugh about this night for the rest of their lives. Maybe they'd find that someone special and lose them in a crowd. (Call me! I'll find them!) Maybe they'd just wake up tomorrow with a nasty hangover and wonder what they had done. Maybe something really bad would happen and they'd regret it (Call my sister; she's a great lawyer!) Or maybe, just maybe, nothing would happen at all.

My place is at the western edge of the Strip, between Sunset and Santa Monica. I own a set of bungalows that I had managed to hold on to on my way down to rock bottom. Most of the people that live there have been there for over a decade. We're like family — in that we merely tolerate each other. It's perfect.

I parked and headed to my place, carrying the sushi plate.

I stopped. The lights were on inside. I chewed my lip, wondering if *I* had left the lights on. I was pretty sure I hadn't. A couple of weeks ago, an ex-girlfriend had dropped by under similar circumstances. Given how that all turned out — very, very ugly, in case you were wondering — I wasn't anxious to see another ex.

A familiar laugh bubbled from inside my bungalow.

*Moe.* I sighed in relief.

Moe is a friend, the only neighbor I more than tolerate, and the manager of the place. It was a position I had been more than happy to give up. He and I are close — both in recovery — but I don't know if we're "Using My Apartment While I'm Gone" close. Especially since his own place is so close by.

I opened the door and found him in his favorite spot on my couch in the middle of my small living room. Moe's a Latino man who claims to be in his early forties, with short, black hair that's starting to go gray. He was wrapped in his favorite floral robe, his legs folded underneath. His eyes darted to me as I stepped in, an apology forming on his face.

For a hot second I wondered what he needed to apologize for — until I saw who had joined him on my couch.

*Paul Cooper* shouted, "Jimmy!" He worked to get himself

up and out of the couch. "You brought food, nice!" He reached for the plate.

I pulled it away. This guy, the worst of the bad pennies.

"What are you doing here, Paul?" I asked as I glided past him, heading to the kitchenette. I put the plate on the counter and glared at him.

Moe raised an eyebrow, realizing he may have gotten involved in something he'd rather not. After all that I had told him, he should've known better. "I found him outside, waiting for you," he explained. "I couldn't leave him standing there."

My face squished. He could've. I stuffed a piece of sushi into my mouth instead of screaming.

Paul did not take the hint. "How did it go?"

"How did it go?" I said in mid-chew. "You mean the party where a coked-up producer wanted to get into the 'Jimmy Cooper business'?"

"He was coked-up?" said Paul.

I nodded, then swallowed what was left in my mouth. "Yeah, and he mentioned having a conversation with you."

At first Paul admitted nothing.

Finally, he said, "Yeah... that might have happened."

"Oh?" I nodded quickly, annoyed. "'*Might* have happened.' I see."

Paul grinned, oblivious. "What did you say? Did you pitch anything? Did it seem — "

"No. No, I did not *pitch* anything," I snapped, reaching for another piece of sushi. There were a lot of emotions to stuff down.

Moe decided to be helpful. "Before this gets more heated, I suggest both of you take a cleansing breath. I can feel the tension rising."

I did not take a cleansing breath.

Paul just looked puzzled.

"OK," said Moe, understanding how this was going to go. He turned to my father. "It was lovely finally meeting you." He offered a hand, which my father took awkwardly. "I see where Jimmy gets his sense of humor." Moe pulled his hand away and said to me, "I need my eight hours, so... Good night." He couldn't get out of there fast enough.

Paul nodded toward Moe's retreating figure. "Good guy."

"Yeah, I know, I've met him before."

"Hah-hah. He's better than a lot of your other friends."

"What are you talking about?"

He stumbled through an answer, "You know, the other friends you hang out with."

"Are you talking about the friends that I had *fifteen* years ago? Because I'm not hanging out with them anymore. You'd know that if — "

"You got anything to drink around here?"

That was a bold move, changing the subject, not to mention what he changed it to. He scoped the place out, looking at the posters of my old movies and some of the memorabilia I had kept.

"I don't drink."

He lifted a shoulder. "Yeah, I know. A beer would be fine." He finger-gunned me and plopped back down on my couch.

I turned to the fridge and grabbed a bottle of water. "This is as strong as it gets around here." I tossed it, and Paul struggled to catch the bottle. It finally landed on the floor at his feet.

He grunted as he leaned forward to pick it up, but he smiled as he straightened, holding the bottle aloft like a trophy. "Not as agile as I used to be."

Paul Cooper had had dreams of being an action star like his hero, Sly Stallone. It didn't work out. Sure, he was in some movies, got some lines and billing. Paul's problem, however, was that he thought he was always at the top of the call sheet — the spot reserved for the *actual* star of the movie — and behaved that way. It was his mantra: "Act like a movie star and the rest will follow."

Spoilers: The rest did not follow.

His career came to a crashing halt when the director and the lead of a direct-to-disc movie had had enough of his attitude and conspired to kill off his character halfway through the shoot.

That's when he turned his sights on managing my career. Thank goodness I was talented enough to get an agent, who took on much of the actual management.

"Tell me about the party." He wiggled his eyebrows in excitement, as he twisted off the bottle cap.

"Why don't you tell *me* how I ended up being there?"

Paul took a chug of water. His face squished as the cold water hit his brain. "I made a few phone calls."

"You did. Why?"

"Why?" he repeated.

"Yeah, Paul. Why? As in, why did you make those phone calls?"

He started, then stopped. Then started again, shrugging. "*This* is an opportunity. I saw you on the news, how you saved that girl. A light bulb went off."

My family refuses to pass up an opportunity to make a buck off my fame. After all, it was also supposed to help keep my mother and sister's law firm from not falling into Chapter 11.

"An opportunity for what?" I asked cautiously.

He took another drink. "Well, me and Maggie — "

"You called Maggie?" I blurted. Maggie was my third and final agent. She was the one who had broken me into movies. She was also the one who had stopped returning my calls. "She's still alive?"

Maggie was pretty old when I started out as her client, and she had smoked well after it had become fashionable to quit.

"She was *thrilled* to hear from me," Paul gloated. "We agreed it would be a great way to relaunch you."

Were they collaborating with Matty's agent, or did all agents have the same three ideas?

"But she said she was out of the game, so..." He pointed to himself. "It's all on me. So I made some calls."

"How many?"

"Calls?"

"Oh, fuck," I mumbled.

Paul put a consoling hand up. "Hey, Jimmy, it only takes one yes to get us back in the game."

"Us?" I wagged my finger, annoyed. "No, no. There is no 'us.'"

"Oh, come on," he said, shifting on the couch. "There's money on the table."

And there it was. Case closed. That was why he was back. Cold, hard cash.

"It'll be like old times," he was saying. He took a look around the small living room before landing on a pizza stain in the carpet that I had never been able to fully get out. "You might even make enough to move to a better place."

"I *like* this place," I said defensively, "and you do know the old times were actually awful, right? Or you *would* if you were actually here for it."

He blushed. "I'm here now."

"Thank God for that." I clapped my hands together. "This

has been fun. And, to be clear, I meant that sarcastically. I've had a long night. I'm going to bed. So..." I pointed to the front door.

Paul didn't move.

I groaned. "What now?"

He gave me a lopsided grin. "Can I crash here? The hotel thinks my credit is no longer good."

He was lying. Either about the credit card or the hotel. If I had to bet, he hadn't been staying at a hotel but had rather worn out his welcome with whoever had been his host. Most likely it was a member of his posse, a collection of has-been actors and stunt men whose raison d'être was to party.

"It's late, and I'm not sure where else I can go," he said.

Shit.

I should've kicked him out, but, regardless of the past, the guy was still my father and a human being.

And Moe would be really disappointed in me if I kicked my father out in a time of need.

I sighed. "You get the couch. And you leave tomorrow."

Not having much of a choice, he agreed to the terms. As I set him up on the couch, I watched him get ready for bed. For a guy who had once been vital, I could see that he was getting older. It wasn't just the dough around his waist; the chest he had been so proud of now sagged too. The only thing intact was his belief that he was still thirty-five and important.

We muttered our good nights, and I went down the hall to my bedroom, thinking about what Paul had said about money and having that nicer place to live. Despite my love for my bungalow, that did sound pretty good. Who wouldn't want a nicer place to live? Maybe with a pool. But was I a pool person? Did I deserve a pool? I shook my head — I did not — and started changing my clothes.

I had money once, lots of money. It didn't do me much good in the long run. Movie-famous money is dangerous in the wrong hands. And Paul's hands were dangerous.

Frankly, so were mine.

I didn't need the money, I told myself; I didn't want the money. I was a private detective now, not an actor, and I was *happy* with that.

Right?

Down to a T-shirt and shorts, I fell into bed. Finally the night was over.

———

FROM A DREAMLESS sleep, my phone woke me. I squinted at the sunlight coming in through my window as I reached for it. Nora was calling. I poked the answer button and said, "It's Sunday, Nora. I thoughts assistants didn't work on Sundays."

"I need you to come into the office," she said. "You have

clients. Their son has been kidnapped."

Finally, some good news. The right kind of case.

# 4
—

TEN MINUTES LATER I was out of my bedroom in a dark blue suit, light orange shirt, and a black tie, standing before my dad — for fuck's sake —*Paul*, as he slept on my couch, partially covered in a summer blanket, shirtless and in his tighty-whities. I shook my head, pushing that nightmare fuel out of my head, and kicked the side of the couch. My guest woke with a jerk.

"What? Who?!"

"I'm going to work," I said.

"It's Sunday," he mumbled, turning away from me.

"Crime doesn't sleep."

"Huh?" He sat up and scratched his belly. "Is there any coffee?"

"Coffee is for closers."

"What?" he asked, not catching my *Glengarry Glen Ross* reference.

"No. There's no coffee. There's a place down the street." I pointed in a vague that-a-way direction. "Nice seeing you," I lied. "You have a safe and quick trip back to Vegas. Moe can lock up."

I didn't wait for a reply.

Moe was outside his place, watering the little garden he had planted around his door. It was a delicious jumble of succulents and cacti, with a dash of flowering plants. He spotted me and straightened to his full height. "My, my, my! Look at you, all dressed up."

"Heading to the office. VIP clients are meeting me there."

"Ooh. VIP?" he said, suggesting that I'd come out and tell him who it was.

I pointed back to my place. "Could you... uh... when he leaves..." I paused. "Can you make sure he *leaves*? Then lock up the place?"

Moe put a hand to his chest. "I feel like this is my fault."

It was.

But I said, "Nooooo! No, of course it's not. Don't worry about it." I waved a goodbye and Moe reluctantly followed suit, still hoping I would spill the beans on the client.

In my car, I headed west toward Century City, listening to "It Never Rains in Southern California" by Albert Hammond.

Metaphor aside, it *does* rain, but you never remember when it did last. The lack of visible change in the seasons creates this illusion that time never passes.

It felt like just last month that Paul Cooper had walked out on our family. Seeing him again (and again), it was like time had collapsed in on itself, and there I was, once again an insecure teenage actor in the midst of a burgeoning drug addiction. My nerves were raw. It would've been better if he had never come back. I had gotten comfortable not even thinking about him.

Not much, anyway.

Besides, I had replaced Paul with a better father figure in Gordon Bixby. Gordon was former LAPD and my mother's in-house detective before me. He was, in fact, my mentor and taught me everything I needed to know before he fucked off into retirement in Colorado. I missed that guy.

We talked occasionally over the phone, but it wasn't the same.

I rolled up in front of the building only five minutes late. Not bad by L.A. standards.

Nora met me in the empty reception area. She tucked her hair behind her ears and then clasped her hands together. "They're in the conference room," she said nervously. They being the potential clients.

"No hellos, no idle chitchat, Nora? Just bang, straight to business?"

She took a quick breath. "The Beverlys are very insistent."

When you're worth billions — yeah, that's right, *billions* — you get to be insistent.

The Beverlys were one of those Old Families of Los Angeles (trademark pending) They were like the oil tycoons, the Dohenys, or the railway barons, the Huntingtons, or the water magnates, the Crosses.

That last one is from *Chinatown*, but you get the idea. The Beverlys were like that, except their money came from real estate holdings they'd snatched up in the early part of the twentieth century. I suppose that made them not exactly *old* old money, but L.A. old all the same.

I followed Nora farther into the very quiet and very empty office. Some places were never meant to be visited after hours, and law offices were one of them.

Nora's eyes darted to me as we approached the conference room. "Have you ever met them before?"

"The Beverlys? Of the Beverly Hills Beverlys?"

Her eyebrows shot up to her forehead.

"Right. No time for jokes. No, I've never met them. They travel in very different circles than us mere mortals."

"I've met millionaires," Nora admitted, "but never billionaires."

I nodded.

If I recalled correctly, the family fortune had started with Ivan Beverly. He had come to America in the 1920's as Ivan

Borokov, and Borokov wasn't exactly a name that was going to inspire trust to Waspy Los Angeles. Everyone was already changing their names to assimilate, to fit into the American Dream — out with Archie Leach, in with Cary Grant — so what was one more? Ivan chose the most aspirational name he could think of. Yep. He literally was a Beverly of Beverly Hills.

Maybe that was the magic sauce, because the dude had a long and wealthy life, turning his real estate fortune into philanthropy. When you have everything, you decide the only thing left to do is buy a good reputation before dying, which is exactly what he'd done by the time he passed away in his late nineties. Everyone respected and loved the guy. Even I knew who he was.

Nora pulled open the glass door to the conference room, and I stepped in.

The Beverlys in question were a husband and wife, sitting on the other side of the long oak table. Robert Beverly didn't need any introduction. He had been in the public eye from the moment he was born. The only son of Ivan, Robert had kicked around the L.A. clubs in his twenties, making the scene while his much older father was still kicking around boardrooms making deals. His family's wealth (and the fact that he came of age before social media) protected him from the worst of public scrutiny, turning facts into unconfirmed stories and then into myths.

"Mr. Cooper," he said, not rising from his seat. What a greeting.

I smiled, grabbed a chair, and put myself in it.

Robert had matured into the billionaire who sat before me, now running a venture capitalist company called The Beverly Group. B- for creativity, A+ for marketing. He was in his fifties now, a dusting of white in his brown hair. He wore a conservative, dark blue, double-breasted suit, gold buttons and all. I guess the gold buttons made up for the lack of a tie, and beneath the suit jacket he wore a crisp, white button-down, opened a button or two more that most would choose. He had a wide face and was trim, not muscular. Probably a golf course kind of guy. He had a deep tan to show for it.

Even with that going for him, he looked like he hadn't slept in days. He had dark rings around his eyes, and his whole face sagged.

"This is my wife, Eva," he said softly.

Like his father, Robert had married a younger second wife before finally settling down and having a kid. Eva was ten years younger than Robert and wore a forest-green suit, finished off with apple-red lipstick and pearl-studded earrings. She was very Euro chic, though her eyes were red, as if she had been crying.

"Thank you for seeing us," she said.

"I got here as soon as I could. Do you need anything?

Water? Coffee?"

Robert waved his hand no for both of them.

Nora sat next to me, ready to take notes, but Mr. Beverly eyed her nervously.

"We want to be assured of the utmost discretion," he said. "This is... it's a difficult situation for us."

"I trust Nora. She's the best," I promised him, then took a breath. "So, your son...?"

"Patrick," said Nora, filling in the blank for me.

"Patrick. He's been kidnapped?" I said, turning back to the Beverlys.

Eva swallowed while Robert nodded. He said. "Yes," he said. "Friday night. We were contacted by email on Saturday in the late afternoon. It contained a video of" — he paused as though he was still processing the whole thing — "two men holding him. Demanding fifty million dollars by Friday."

Less than a week from now. I nodded. Every parent's nightmare.

"Could you even get that much in that time?"

Robert crossed his arms. "Of course." He was practically insulted by the suggestion he couldn't do it. "But they want it in diamonds."

Fifty million dollars in diamonds. I fought the urge to whistle. That would be a move up in the world for a lot of people.

"We didn't believe it at first," Eva said. "It must be a joke, or something. We tried calling Patrick. We sent Edward to his home…" Her voice cracked, though, and she couldn't finish.

"Edward?" I prompted.

Robert answered, "Edward Stratton, he's in charge of security for the family. He recovered security footage showing Patrick being taken from the home we rented for his while he attended USC. This was Friday night. Edward recommended we reach out to you; he felt it would be best if you handled the case."

Looked like I had a fan out there.

"Were there any threats or anything? Anyone suspicious hanging around?"

Eva shook her head no. Robert said, "Given who we are, we're always under threat; there's always someone suspicious. But it's never anything serious."

Uh-huh.

"I'd like to talk to Edward," I said. "He could tell me all the not serious threats he's aware of."

"Of course," said Robert.

"Who's the detective handling the case?"

*Please don't be her, please don't be her*, I was chanting to myself when I realized there was no answer to my question. There was only deep silence as Robert and Eva looked at Nora.

I did the same.

Nora put her pen down. "They haven't gone to the police."

My soul left my body, and I wondered why Nora hadn't filled me on that detail from the beginning. Everything was quiet. Time had stopped. I simply could not believe what I had heard. This was playing with fire, this not calling the police. From a long way away, I managed to speak. "Did the kidnappers say not to go to the police? Because, spoilers, they always say that."

Then it occurred to me why the Beverlys may have made this choice. And I didn't want to be right. "Is this about discretion?"

Robert answered, "If we went to the police and it somehow got to the media, it could create chaos. And in that chaos, anything could happen to Patrick."

"He's our only child," said Eva quietly.

Discretion it was. I took a deep breath, my mind and body beginning to reunite. Another thing I wouldn't be able to share with Ito.

"Patrick means the world to us. Keeping this contained, we feel" — he glanced at his wife, who didn't look like she was in total agreement — "is the best way to bring him home alive."

The two of them looked so alone, each sitting there, next to each other, dealing with this shit in their own way.

The cold pit in my stomach remained. "All right. But I just want it" — I looked at Nora — "on the record that I really think it's a terrible idea."

"Noted," said Robert said tersely.

I took a breath, shrugged defensively. "With all due respect, have you considered just... paying them off? Fifty million is like a rounding error for you."

"Because if we pay them off," snapped Robert, "what's the guarantee that he'll come home alive?"

"What if he's dead already?" said Eva added. "Or hurt? He needs us to find him."

In most cases, kidnappers need and want their victims alive. They're already on the hook for the kidnapping — a federal crime — and they don't want to add to the charges. But then again, the victim could also become a witness that points them out in a lineup, so...

"The police — " I started.

"*Enough* with the police." Robert looked at his wife and then dug his eyes deep into me. "I'm beginning to wonder if you're the man for this job."

I began to sweat. "Mr. Beverly, I'm just — " I stopped myself. They just weren't getting it. "A week isn't a lot of time."

Robert was about to say something, but Eva put her hand on his and his mouth shut. "We understand, Mr. Cooper. We're a family with resources, and we're asking you to do your very best."

"And I will," I said.

She nodded in agreement. "Patrick, for someone born into such wealth" — that's a word for it — "he's really down to earth."

Robert grunted and moved in his chair. I guess he didn't approve of being down to earth.

Eva continued. "During this summer break from school, he was looking into working with some charities." She looked to her husband. "He hadn't decided on anything yet, but..." She turned to me. "He's kind. He gets along with everyone. He tries to make people feel special."

I got that. When I was at the height of my fame, I would go out of my way to make people feel comfortable around me and my success. Maybe it was out of a sense of guilt that, yeah, I could buy almost anything I wanted at sixteen years old, and here I was meeting a kid who had to mow lawns to get the Air Jordans his parents couldn't afford. Patrick was doing the same thing.

So when I heard that story about Patrick "looking into working with some charities...." Sure, my man. Sure you are.

"He's a bit of a dreamer," said Robert with finality. Maybe that was Dad-speak for "unserious."

I nodded, taking that in, his choice of words, his tone of voice. Robert and Patrick were not on the same team, the feeling in my head buzzed, even if they shared the same last name.

"OK," I said. "I'll find him."

# 5

—

"I FOUND HIM!" I said, sitting at my desk, L.A. stretching out behind me. Mr. and Mrs. Beverly had left about twenty minutes ago, after giving Nora and me more information on Patrick and his friends. A meeting with their security guy, Edward Stratton, had been set up over at Patrick's house in Silver Lake.

"You what?" said Nora, stepping into my office with a cup of coffee.

I held up my phone. "Online. I found him... Sorry, I should've led with that. I found his socials."

She took a deep breath and cradled the mug, trying to calm her rattled nerves. Together we had watched the hostage video the kidnappers had sent the Beverlys. It wasn't pretty.

From a fade-in, there he was, Patrick Beverly, age twenty, blondish in the glare of the overly bright lighting. He had been placed in a chair in front of a white wall with no pictures and, of course, no distinguishing marks. He looked to be healthy and in good shape, in that way twenty-somethings have, if you ignored the fact that he was also duct-taped to a folding chair and looked terrified. His eyes were wet and pleading as he sucked on a ball gag. Very *Pulp Fiction*.

"We have your son." The voice was filtered and loud, as if the kidnapper was eating the microphone. "Fifty million dollars in diamonds will get you his safe return." A figure in black with a leather mask — they were really going for a whole BDSM thing, huh? — stepped into frame and grabbed Patrick's hair, pulling his head back. He placed a knife to the kid's throat. The voice continued, "You have until Friday. We will contact you two hours before the exchange with a location. Do not call the authorities. Do not fuck with us."

And that was that. The screen had gone black, and I had looked over at Nora. She tapped a finger to her lips; she was barely breathing.

"I'm sorry," I said. "Maybe I should've watched it alone."

She snapped out of it. "It's... You see these sort of things in movies all the time, and, you know, you don't think about how they could be real and..."

"Yeah." I had closed the file on my computer. "Go take a break."

She didn't move.

"We're going to find him," I assured her.

"That's what you said to them."

"And I believe it."

"How can you be so sure?" she asked.

I honestly didn't have an answer for her, but I gave her my best reassuring smile. After she left, I decided it was time to look at the security footage from Patrick's house the night he was taken. The clip showed Patrick walking up to his place on Friday evening. Just as he got to his door, a large man — bulkier than the guy in the video — stepped up from behind Patrick. He pulled the kid back, a handkerchief over his nose and mouth. And then they were gone, leaving nothing but a grim, black door in the security camera's frame.

It was done in seconds. These guys — at least two of them — were experienced. Patrick hadn't heard his kidnapper coming, and the other must've have been waiting in some sort of vehicle to carry him away.

I took a cleansing breath and turned to Patrick's socials.

The coffee in Nora's hand actually smelled good, which confused me. The coffee that came out of the Cooper and Associates break room was traditionally terrible. I looked back at my phone and said to her, "I think I'm beginning to like this kid."

Patrick Beverly — I don't think there could have been a

name any further from Ivan's cold Russian winters — was in his junior year at USC, studying communications. His father had rolled his eyes when Eva told me that. Patrick got decent grades, texted his parents, and, scrolling through his socials, he seemed to have a great life. Lots of friends. It helped that he was rich, sure, but Patrick had a warm smile. And maybe I'm a sucker for a warm smile.

"Jimmy," said Nora firmly, snapping me out of my reverie.

I looked up from my phone, then remembered, "Right, I have to go over to Patrick's — "

"Your mother is here."

I stopped in the middle of getting up. "What?" I sat back down.

"Your mother is — "

"Here. OK. That's what I thought you said."

"She'd like to speak to you." Nora took a sip of her coffee. "In her office."

Greta Cooper, my mother, was here on a Sunday. Was that extraordinary? I didn't know. I never came in on a Sunday. Maybe Mom was always here.

I nodded to Nora and headed to my mother's office. On the way, I wondered why she might want to see me about. She hadn't handled my solving the big case very well, and I had kept out of her way for the past week. She had fully expected me to fuck things up, but then, lo and behold, her son had pulled out a win. She probably thought it might all go to my head and make me unbearable.

Spoilers: She was probably right.

I stopped in the hall, halfway there. Or maybe she knew Paul was in town.

Shit.

Greta Cooper also had a corner office, this one with a view of the Hollywood Hills. She sat at her desk, reading glasses perched at the end of her nose, reviewing a case file. She was dressed as casualy as I had ever seen her in this office, in a cream-colored blouse and navy blue slacks. The pearls around her neck added that dash of class she wouldn't leave home without.

I knocked on the doorframe and decided my best defense was to dazzle her. "You'll *never* believe who I signed as a client. You're going to be impressed."

She looked up, pulled her reading glasses off, and folded them. "You mean the Beverlys, James?" She leaned back, secretly enjoying herself.

I folded my arms, immediately disappointed. "Nora told you?"

"Of course."

I noticed on the side table along the wall beneath a large abstract painting, a cardboard coffee traveler from one of Century City's more upscale cafes, holding enough have to get twenty people wired. Well, when it came to the origin of Nora's coffee, and it's quality, mystery solved.

And I also now knew Nora's price to spill the beans.

"They really don't want to go to the police?" she said.

I shook my head.

She sighed. "While it's not illegal, their choice, it is…"

"Stupid?" I suggested.

She blinked. "I was going to say dangerous."

"I told them that." I shook my head. "They're risking their son."

Mom shook her head. "I meant for you. It's dangerous for *you*."

I frowned. "You mean, it's dangerous for *him*. He's the one that's, you know, kidnapped."

She leaned forward. "Of course he's in danger, James. But the Beverlys are putting you in the line of fire as well. They get everything they want — privacy — and if it goes wrong, they have someone to blame."

She didn't have to say who.

I rocked back and forth on the balls of my feet. "I guess we'll just have to make sure nothing goes wrong."

"*James*," she said, annoyed. I assumed that she wished Gordon Bixby was handling this important case. But he wasn't here. I was.

"Come on, Mother. You gotta give me the benefit of the doubt. Right?"

She paused, considered my track record. "I do. I actually do." She nodded.

Stop the press, Vicki Vale. My mother was giving me props. In her own, special way.

"I'm worried," she said, looking away. "I'm uncomfortable with the bargain."

Whoa. She actually was worried.

"You want me to quit?"

She glanced up at me.

"Oh, no. Of course not. We'll be charging them a lovely retainer for your services, and perhaps they can take advantage of our other legal services as well." She tapped a finger on her desk. "Besides, I would rather you focus on a case."

Pause. What did she mean by "rather"? Rather than what? Working on a case *rather than* hiding your father from me? Was that what she meant? I thought about asking her. Sure, I would get some clarity and I would know if she knew my father was in town, even if she tried to lie to me. But then, if she *didn't* know, she would ask why I was asking, and then would I be able to come up with an airtight lie that would convince her to stop asking?

Spoilers: I would not.

Best to just play her game.

"Right. Better working a case than wasting time here at the office."

A thin smile. "Yes. Wasting time at the office. Did you think I meant something else?"

At that point, I couldn't tell you which way was up. She was a master at this game.

"Nope!" I said overly loud, ready to get out out of her office. I turned and headed to the door.

"James."

I stopped and turned.

"Regardless of their motivations for sticking your neck out, the Beverlys are important. They are the biggest clients we've ever had walk through our doors. I'd like to keep them. Please act professional." She paused. "As much as you understand professionalism."

I smiled, finger-gunned, and left.

Fifteen minutes later, I was in my car, heading east on Santa Monica Boulevard, followed by an easy right onto Beverly Boulevard while in Beverly Hills, blasting Harvey Danger's "Flagpole Sitta" as loudly as my speakers were able. I sang along as I headed to Silver Lake, where the Beverlys had rented a place for Patrick while he studied at USC. Not exactly close to the campus, but way cooler.

It was easy to weave through the Sunday traffic, and it suited my mood. The conversation with my mom had unnerved me. I didn't like the position the clients had put me in — especially after Mom confirmed to me how serious the consequences could be — and I didn't like not knowing whether Mom knew Paul Cooper was in town or not. I thought about just coming clean with her, but then again,

Paul was leaving today and I could get away with it.

Focus. I had to focus. There was a kid out there who needed me.

The neighborhood wrapped around the Silver Lake Reservoir, built by William Mulholland because the desert basin that is L.A. needed a steady supply of water. (See? *Chinatown* is not only a great movie, but a piece of history.) It's one of those hip and cool places to live and hang out.

Of course, the movie nerd in me loves it because it's where Laurel and Hardy tried to wrestle a piano up an impossibly long flight of stairs.

To be honest, even after reviewing the kidnapping footage and Patrick's socials, I had very little to start this case on. I hoped the Beverlys' security guy could give me a lead, and as such, I wondered what sort of person I was going to be working with. Would he want to be in charge, giving out orders? I did not want to deal with some Alpha Dude. But then, he *had* recommended me to his clients. He couldn't be all bad.

Beverly Boulevard turned into Silver Lake Boulevard, and Prince's "Pop Life" started as I hit the reservoir. I turned left and went up and around, the roads getting narrower and the real estate prices going up as I climbed.

The house the Beverlys had rented for their son, a Spanish Revival from the 1920s, was built on a hillside, and I doubted there was much of a backyard. I bet there was a hot tub, though. I parked on the very steep, very short driveway next to a polished, dark blue BMW. Classy. Must have been Edward's car. I paused in front of the house's black front door, and a shiver passed through me. Right here was where it happened. A few days ago, Patrick stood here, coming home, and he didn't hear someone coming behind him. It felt... well, it felt like visiting those steps where Laurel and Hardy kept losing the piano. Discordant. Like stepping into something unreal.

A slow-moving cyclist plugged away, heading up the hill. He was in his fifties, gasping for air. He looked at me through those dumb wraparound sunglasses.

I waved.

The cyclist nodded as he kept gasping and pedaling.

He was probably going to live forever while I would be lucky to make it pasty forty.

I jumped as the front door opened.

# 6

—

A THIN MAN In his forties with a shaved head looked me up and down. He was pale, which contrasted sharply with his black suit. He looked like the kind of guy who got in ten miles on the treadmill before his protein shake each morning.

"Jimmy Cooper." There was a dash of disappointment in his voice. Normally it takes some time for me to disenchant people.

"The one and only," I said, smiling and stepping into the house. "What do I call you? Ed? Eddie? Edward? That feels really — "

"Stratton," he said, indifferent.

"Oh. OK. A just-the-last-name type. Cool. Very *cool*," I

said.

It was not cool.

I wondered *why* he was being so uncool. Given that he was the one who recommended me to the Beverlys, where was my warm reception?

I looked around the place, left and right. The home was a classic with its beamed ceilings and terra-cotta floors. It had been lovingly kept up.... until a twenty-year-old moved in.

To my right was a living room that featured the largest TV a billionaire's son could buy, with game controllers chaotically littered across the coffee table in front of the brown leather couch. Pizza boxes dotted the landscape, though they were eclipsed by a Chinese takeout mountain. A couple of shrines to exotic fruit-flavored soda had been built here and there. And, there it was, the smell of weed in the air — thick and skunky, something that wasn't going to be Febrezed away.

"Someone's not getting their deposit back," I said conspiratorially.

Stratton cocked his head, not playing along. "I was told you wanted to look around," he said.

I nodded, smiled again, and said, "Yeah, you know... look for evidence. Clues."

He folded his arms. "You saw the security footage?"

"I did. Scary."

Stratton bobbed his head. "And you think there's something to be gained from searching the house?"

"I didn't say *search*, but yeah. Maybe there's something here. Maybe Patrick put on a Post-it, 'I was being followed by a black van with no windows.'"

Stratton frowned. "Patrick didn't leave any Post-its."

"Well, *yeah.*" I snorted. "I don't really think there's one."

"Then why did you say it?"

I paused. Had Stratton been born without a sense of humor or did he just have it removed? "You got me there." I pointed at the stairs. "Can you show me the rest of the house?"

He smoldered, then said, "Upstairs there's three bedrooms and two baths." He turned and led me up.

It suddenly felt like I was with the worst real estate agent in L.A. I imagined Stratton's pitch as he showed me through the house: *This is a home. It overlooks Silver Lake. It contains three bedrooms, and a Jack and Jill bathroom. Perfect for not fully formed humans. Did I neglect to mention the newly renovated master bathroom? Well, there is. I have been told it is tastefully done. Out back there is a hot tub in a truly secure backyard.*

Sold.

Looking around, what got to me, was how *clean* upstairs was compared to downstairs. The master suite, sure, it was lived in — Patrick had a closet full of graphic Ts and hoodies

— but it was neat and orderly. The bed was even made.

Who was this kid?

As I snooped through a chest of drawers, not finding anything salacious, much less suspicious, I said to Stratton, "Tell me more about Patrick."

Stratton put his hands behind his back and said nothing.

"You do *know* Patrick, don't you?"

"Of *course* I do," he replied, like I had asked the dumbest question possible. "I've been with the family for years."

"Then tell me about him." I closed the drawer I had been poking around in and leaned against the chest. "I need a feel for the guy. What was he like? Did he get along with his parents?"

"What does that have to do with him being taken?"

I took a breath and pushed it out. "OK, look. What's going on?"

"What do you mean?"

I pointed at myself. "You... you did recommend me to the Beverlys, right? You told them to hire me?"

He swallowed and said, "Yeah," like he was a petulant teen who had been caught stealing.

I gave him a healthy dose of side-eye. He was telling me the truth, and I was still confused.

"Patrick's a good kid," he said. "From what I see. I don't spend a lot of time with him."

That wasn't entirely true, but the guy was probably

protecting Patrick. Stratton was, after all, hired to safeguard the family, and that included its secrets.

"He gets good grades. Keeps his nose clean."

I nodded like I was buying it.

He went on to tell me that Patrick hadn't seen anything weird or suspicious in the days leading up to his kidnapping. He said that he'd gone through all the security camera's footage he could get his hands on and still hadn't seen anything himself. This led him to believe that the kidnappers were well organized and good at their work. He shook his head. "Someone like Patrick never stood a chance."

I agreed. "Do you think this was personal?"

"What do you mean?"

I shrugged. "I mean, do you think there's more to this than just profit? There are tons of wealthy kids to kidnap in L.A. Why Patrick?"

Stratton didn't have any idea. Maybe he was in the wrong line of work. Which begged the question: "Why aren't you the one leading the case?"

I could see how uncomfortable my question made him.

"Why me instead of you?" I prodded. "I would think that, you know, this would be in your wheelhouse."

"Well," he said, licking his lips, "maybe because he was taken, it wasn't so much in my wheelhouse. And..." He stopped. "I just thought I should fall on my sword. Take the blame. Let someone else find him."

Which wasn't quite the truth, but I wondered if Mr. Beverly had been the one to ask Stratton to fall on his sword, but I left it at that.

I checked out the other bedrooms. In one, Patrick had quite the computer setup. Three screens, great speakers, and a high-end desktop. I poked at the keyboard. The screen came to life and asked for a password. I typed PASSWORD to be a bit of a dick. Maybe I'd get lucky. I did not.

I looked at Stratton, who hovered in the doorway. "You know the password?"

He shook his head. "Patrick didn't like to share. He didn't like the idea of me being able to snoop in on his business." He paused. "I can get one of the Beverlys' IT guys to look into it."

The other bedroom looked to be a guest room that no one stayed in.

Giving up on the idea of finding some secret clue to the kidnappers' identities, I led Stratton back down into the first-floor mess.

Over my shoulder, I said, "Mr. and Mrs. Beverly mentioned threats."

"Oh, yes. They get them quite regularly."

"You never did anything about them?"

He cleared his throat. I was veering into unwelcome territory. "For the most part, they are cranks and crazies. Those that we assessed to be real threats, something that might have real action behind them, we forwarded those to the police."

"And...?"

"You'd have to ask them."

Which I couldn't because the Beverlys wanted discretion.

"Right." We reached the front door, and I turned to him. "Could you send me a list of those threats? Just in case?"

A slight shrug and a nod as he showed me out to the porch. "I could put something together." He closed the door behind us, punched in a code and the deadbolt slid into place.

As he headed to his car, I said, "OK, this has been great! We should do it again sometime."

He stood next to his car, frowned, confused, a man utterly bereft of a sense of humor. "Call my office if you come up with anything." He slipped on some shades. "Day or night."

"Got it. Hey..." I called. Stratton stopped. "How do you think Patrick's holding up?"

Stratton said nothing. Then: "He'll make it. He's got reserves no one knows about."

Huh.

Without so much as a goodbye, Stratton got into his BMW and headed downhill to my left. It made me think. Down would have been the quickest way back to West Silver Lake Drive. I looked to my right; the kidnappers could've gone up and around. It might have been slower, but less suspicious.

I took a step off the stoop and walked to the edge of the driveway.

And they would have to have staked out the place so they could get an idea of Patrick's comings and goings.

Even then... the street was narrow and had limited parking. If they were staking out the place, someone had to have seen something.

A lot for the kidnappers to consider.

Just then, a round, short white woman in her sixties in a mint-green windbreaker strode down around the curve of the street. One arm pumped while the other held the leash to a large, black dog.

I grinned and waved at her. She nodded but didn't slow.

People in L.A. aren't going to stop and talk to just anyone with a smile. You'll only get stuck in a weird conversation. Which I was about to have with this woman.

"Excuse me?" I called.

She was about to pass but slowed, looking at me with a wary *Hmmmm?* expression on her face. Even the dog regarded me with circumspection.

"How are you?" I asked, which could have been the worst opening ever.

She nodded. She also kept pumping her legs up and down. Everyone in this neighborhood was intent on living forever.

"You live around here?" Oh, man. Did I just get creepier?

She slowed in her steps and didn't answer. The dog took a

greater interest in me, moving toward my feet and sniffing. Look, dogs are cute, but they're cuter over there, not up close and personal.

"Do I know you?" she asked, and then recognition dawned. "Oh! I've seen you on TV! You're that detective guy."

See? *That's* how a fan is supposed to greet you. "I am." Now that she knew who I was, hopefully this conversation would be easier.

She beamed. "What do you know? I am meeting a *real* celebrity."

"Thank you," I said, though maybe now she was the one taking things a little far. "I'm wondering, have you seen anything strange lately?"

"Huh. Well, I did see Elton John in the freezer section at Bristol Farms in Beverly Hills about a year ago."

I shook my head. That was on me. I didn't think I needed to be more specific. "I meant here," I explained. "On this street. Maybe in front of this house?"

Still moving, she put a hand to her lips. "Nothing *strange* strange. I think a young man lives here. He likes to throw parties." She shook her head with disdain.

I leaned closer and said, "You look like you know everyone around here."

She took it as intended, a compliment to her ego. "I do like to keep an eye on things."

"No one just sitting in their cars?"

She scowled. "That *would* be strange. And I said, I haven't seen anything strange." She paused. "Did something happen? Am *I* a part of an investigation?"

I put a finger to my lips. "Top secret."

She shivered with excitement, then crowed to her dog, "You hear that, Cookie? Top secret."

I gave her my card. "If you think of anything…"

"I will give you a call." She beamed and tugged at the leash. "Let's go." She and her dog headed on down the hill.

*No stakeouts*, I thought. They must've tracked Patrick some other way. By his phone? Did they hack his schedule?

I dropped into my car. The next logical step would be to hit up Patrick's friends. Maybe they had seen something or he had said something to them. I cross-referenced the list the Beverlys had given me with Patrick's social media to see who he had been hanging out with recently.

My phone beeped in my hand. A text. My heart beat faster as I saw it was from Detective Violet Ito, LAPD, Robbery-Homicide. The very same detective that I had worried might be on this case, the very same woman I had chosen *not* to hang out with in favor of that stupid party last night in the Hollywood Hills.

*Sup?* she texted.

*Are you asking in an official capacity?* I replied with a winking emoji.

She and I, well… I didn't know what we were. We had met

on my last case, and, at least in my opinion, there was a strong will-they-won't-they vibe between us.

*I am not*, she texted. *Just making sure you're not getting into trouble.*

*Me? Never.* I grinned as I settled back against my headrest. We were totally flirting. Over text. We were flexting. It's what the kids are calling it.

Spoilers: They are not and will never be calling it that.

Their loss.

*Hey*, I typed, *professional question: have you ever worked a missing persons case?* I hit send before realizing my mistake.

The bubbles on my screen danced. Stopped. Then danced again. Stopped.

My phone rang. A video call. From her.

After contemplating not answering — which would be pretty suspicious — I picked up the call.

Her face appeared on the screen. Violet Ito was in her late twenties, Japanese-American, with shoulder-length black hair. She was calling from her desk, and I could see the rest of the Robbery-Homicide bullpen behind her.

"Are you working a case, Jimmy?" she said before I could say hello.

"A case?" I paused. I had told the Beverlys I would be discreet. So I sorta had to be discreet and hope it wouldn't blow up in my face. "Nah. Just curious."

She examined me closely. I wasn't sure if she was buying

it or not. "Curious?"

I shook her question off. "Someone asked me about it." I hoped she couldn't see me blush. My face felt like it was on fire.

"Uh-huh."

I tried laughing. "Could kidnapping be considered robbery?" I kept laughing through my poor attempt at a joke.

"Are you OK, Jimmy?" She looked deeper into her screen. "Where are you?"

"I'm great, I am great. Just running errands." Change the subject! "I'm sorry about last night." Perfect. Apologizing meant I didn't have to keep lying about what I was doing."Can I make up for it? Coffee sometime this week?"

A gruff voice shouted from behind her, "Would you stop talking to your boyfriend? Paperwork's not going to finish itself." Her partner, Kemble, was drowning in it, I guessed.

She turned to the off-camera voice. "Shut up. I've already done my half." She rolled her eyes and said to me, "Coffee's great. If you need anything..."

I grinned. "I got it. Maybe midweek?"

"Sounds good."

Kemble grumbled again, "Ito, get off the damn — "

She mouthed a "bye" and hung up.

I took a deep breath and started my car. Harry Styles's "Sign of the Times" started up. I headed down the street, driving back home to West Hollywood, where I could plan out my next steps in some peace and quiet.

# 7
—

"WHY ARE YOU still *here*?" I snarled to my father. He stood in the middle of my living room, the exact spot he wasn't supposed to be in. He should've been in his car or, better yet, back in Vegas. Anywhere else but right in front of me.

"I felt we had some unfinished business," he declared, puffing his chest.

"Oh, you did, did you?"

"There's a lot to talk about," he countered.

I was baffled. After more than a decade, suddenly he thought we had a lot to talk about.

"So, you know, I thought I should stay," he finished lamely, his chest beginning to deflate.

I put my foot down. "I can't have you here, Paul. I'm in

the middle of a case."

"Oh, I don't mind."

He didn't mind?

"When you're not working 'the case,' we can — "

"Why did you say it like that? It's an *actual* case. I am actually a detective." I turned and headed to my refrigerator. Feeling things made me thirsty.

"Sure," he offered.

*Daggers*. From my eyes.

Paul put up his hands in defense. "OK, OK. You're a detective with a case. Better?"

"No," I said, cracking a water bottle open. "Because you're still here." I drank. "Why are you still here?"

"I've made some calls — "

"More calls? You made *more*? Why would you do that?"

"Because, Jimmy, as I said before, there's an opportunity here."

"I don't need an opportunity, Paul. I'm in a really good place."

He shifted his feet and slipped his hands in his pockets. He sort of groaned and sniffed, then grunted, "I'm not. In a good place."

That knocked me back on my heels. From past experience, I knew Paul had a hard time admitting that.

"OK," I mumbled, unsure where this confession was leading.

With a half-smile he said, "I could really use an opportunity. Just to kinda get back on stable ground." He looked at me with his puppy-dog eyes.

And, *dammit*, if I didn't feel something for him. This could not stand. Shaking my head, I stormed past him and out of my place. I crossed the way and started pounding on Moe's door, shouting his name. I kept at it until he opened. "You had *one* job," I accused him by way of greeting.

He stood there, arms folded, in a white T and blue jeans, his lips twisted in annoyance. Behind him, on the couch, was a guy I had seen leaving his place about two weeks ago. Handsome, quite a catch, and I guess not the one night stand I thought he had been. He looked annoyed too.

I had interrupted something.

I charged ahead. "Moe — "

He put a finger to my chest and pushed. I took a couple of steps back. Over his shoulder, he said, "I'll be right back. Help yourself to more cookies."

I saw the guy reach for the plate as Moe closed the door.

"First," he began, "do not pound on my door. You're a human being; you can knock."

"*Moe* — "

"Not done, honey. Second, I get that you're upset, but that doesn't mean you disrespect me." He put his hand down.

"Are you done?" I ventured, some of the wind knocked out of my sails.

"I am. Now, what is it that you want to discuss?"

I pointed at my place. "He was supposed to be gone. I asked you to make sure he left. He's still there."

Moe agreed. "He didn't want to go."

"Right. I get that. But it's *my* place. You're the manager. Manage him."

Moe put a hand back up, and I shut up.

"Unless you want me to call the cops, there's very little I can do. I know he triggers you," he said. "I can see that. I see the state you're in."

"I'm not in a state."

Moe crossed his arms and tetched. "Oh, honey."

OK. Yeah. I was totally in a state.

"Think of this as an opportunity," said Moe.

"I'm a little full on opportunities right now," I mumbled. Everyone kept telling me I was missing out on an opportunity for this or for that. It was all making me wonder if I really was missing out on something better when, in fact, I had it pretty good. Didn't I?

"You have an opportunity," Moe emphasized, "to really wrap up the past. How often does that come along?"

"Too often."

Moe raised an eyebrow, not appreciating my bon mot. He was right, though. *Ugh.*

He glanced over at my place and then down at his feet. "I don't know what to tell you. The man is a weight around your neck."

"Because he's here. In my face."

Moe shook his head. "It's not just that he's here *now*. He's always been a weight around your neck. He hung it on you the moment he walked out the door."

I fought the urge to run screaming into traffic. "He's here *now* and he wants help."

"Sounds like you're both on a journey."

Sometimes I hated conversations with Moe. It was like he could reach into my psyche with a fork and pluck out the juiciest, most insightful thing and wave it around.

"So, what, he and I go to therapy together?"

"Or go to a meeting."

Moe and I both chuckled at the idea of Paul Cooper at an AA meeting. He would probably roll up and wonder which bar everyone was going to meet up at after.

"I get it," Moe said. "If it was my father…" He looked up and away, his head wobbling. He bit his lip, lost in thought. A quick breath brought him back to me. "I don't know if I could do what I'm asking you to do. But the story of our lives is to become better people."

I wondered if he meant *me* being a better person or me helping Paul become a better person.

"And if this means reconciling" — he put up a hand, anticipating my objection — "or at least making peace with your father, that's a journey worth going on."

So, me. He meant me becoming a better person. Shit.

"Sorry about" — I waved my hand toward his door — "interrupting."

His eyes twinkled. "Nothing was interrupted that can't be restarted. You have a good night."

"You too."

Moe grinned, turned, and headed back inside, offering his date an apology in Spanish.

I looked back at my place. A surge of hot guilt flooded my body. To be clear, it wasn't because I suddenly felt *bad* for my father. I felt bad for how I had behaved. This moment, along with all the others, was on him being a lousy father, a lousier manager, and on him walking out, leaving me with so many questions.

And there it was: the weight around my neck.

I carried it across the way, back to my place. Inside, Paul was in the kitchen, staring into the fridge. Hearing me come in, he turned. "You have no food in here."

"Yeah?"

"Well, what are we going to eat for dinner?" he said, assuming he was staying.

And I guess he was.

"We'll order out." Look at me, solving the big problems.

"Pizza?" he asked with the enthusiasm of a five-year-old.

Thirty minutes later, a pepperoni pizza arrived, and after convincing Paul that he could have water with his dinner or nothing, I put on *Commando* for him to watch while I worked and ate.

Frankly, I was relieved that I could punt being a "better person" to maybe tomorrow.

Paul sprawled on the couch, bare feet on the coffee table. He ate while watching Ah-nold work his screen magic as I sat in my recliner, cracking open on my tablet the files that Nora had emailed about the Beverlys.

"Are you reading?" asked Paul. "You're missing the movie."

"I've seen it," I sighed, not looking up from Nora's meticulously outlined memo.

He pointed at the screen with a slice of pizza. "You're gonna miss the dead tired line. It's the best line in the movie."

I looked up at the screen just in time to see Arnold snap the neck of his would-be hostage taker just before takeoff on a flight bound for South America. He covered him with a hat and blanket before asking a stewardess not to disturb his friend because he's, you know..."Dead tired." Paul chuckled at the line. I smiled. It was so dumbly iconic.

And you gotta love a movie where Schwarzenegger plays a guy named *Matrix*. Oh, the 1980s.

I turned my attention back to the file.

Nora was thorough in her background on the Beverly family. She even included a rumor about the source of Ivan

Beverly's fortune. The rumor had it that during World War II, when Japanese Angelinos were being rounded up and sent to internment camps, he swooped in and bought up their homes, later reselling them for quite a profit.

Pretty sure that tidbit wasn't in the *L.A. Times* obit when Ivan died. Of course, that wouldn't be the first ugly beginning to a family fortune in this town.

Meanwhile, Paul was throwing jabs and taking the punches right along with Arnold during a fight scene. I respected how deeply he felt when he watched his action movies. He wanted to be right in on the action just as much as he was watching it.

I pulled my attention away from the movie and back to my homework. While his father had made a fortune in real estate, Robert Beverly had made his by being on the forefront of the digital one. He had been at the right place at the right time when the internet exploded. It wasn't luck or savvy that made his fortune, but rather having a fortune to begin with. This helped him to spread out his bets. Robert Beverly only needed a few wins to cover the losses of the others.

Ultimately, the son outshone the father, becoming a multibillionaire.

Robert had met his first wife, Ryane, a good Irish girl, in college. Things didn't work out, and she took her healthy divorce settlement back east. She had remarried with kids, and worked in the C-suites of corporate America. Sounded like things had worked out for her.

Eva came into the picture a little more than twenty years ago, having been set up on a date with Robert.

My eyes kept drifting back to the movie.

I was probably ten, maaaaaaaaybe eleven the first time Paul showed me *Commando*. I was home from school, having left early to go on a commercial audition. *Commando* is not a movie for kids. It's not *Kindergarten Cop* or *Jingle All the Way*. It is a hyper-violent, super-masculine action flick that Mom would *never* have approved of me watching. But she was at work, and I was at home with my ne'er-do-well father. I don't remember where Erika was. Maybe she was at a friend's house after school. As we watched, I quickly realized two things. One: I was going to be the coolest kid at school when I described every moment of this movie, and two: at no time could I ever tell my mom that I had seen it.

I hit the section of Nora's notes about Patrick. Good grades, good kid, blah, blah, blah. I closed the folder and watched the rest of the movie.

Once Arnold had killed the last bad guy in the most cinematic way possible — death by steam pipe — my father turned to me and asked, "Another? *Raw Deal?* We should watch *Raw Deal*." He reached for the remote.

"Tempting." I pushed myself out of my recliner. "But it's late and I have work."

"Come on, Jimmy." He gestured to the TV. "We always do a double feature."

We did. That's true.

But I was feeling the past few days catching up with me and Patrick was out there, somewhere, needing my help. "I really can't. Maybe tomorrow."

He nodded, disappointed.

"You need anything?" I said.

He shook his head no.

I nodded. "Listen. About the calls and the meetings and stuff..."

"Yeah?" he said, hopefully.

"If it's..." I couldn't believe I was even saying it. "If it's something interesting — "

"Something *interesting*. Of course."

He was getting ahead of himself.

I held up a cautionary hand. "I'll *think* about it."

He grinned. He had won. At least for the moment. "I promise you, I will only bring interesting things to you. I've been running a comedy club in Vegas. I know what's interesting."

"You run a *comedy* club?"

He shrugged. "It's something I fell into. It's a long story."

Of course he was going to leave out the important details.

"The thing is," he went on, "I was pretty good at it. For awhile, anyway, but... it's on the shit end of the Strip."

"It's Vegas. How can you tell?"

He laughed, nodded. "That's good, that's good. Maybe I should book you."

"I work hourly now."

"So does a lot of entertainment in Vegas."

It was my turn to laugh. I could see the relief on my father's face. Someone thought he was funny. "So, Jimmy, I'm not asking for a handout or anything. I just... I'm asking for a chance for you and me to work together, you know? I want to earn my keep."

That was his whole pitch. And he was telling me the truth.

I gave a one shoulder-shrug. "OK."

He brightened. "This is great. You'll see. We'll see if we can make each other rich."

"Sure." My lips smushed together as I nodded. I turned and headed down the hall to my bedroom, saying over my shoulder, "Night, Dad."

# 8

—

"BACK UP. *WHAT?*" Erika said. She was standing in the middle of my office and speaking a little too loudly.

I bounded across the room and closed my door. I repeated myself, more quietly. "Dad — *Paul* — is at my place."

My sister put her fists on her hips. Oh, shit. I was in trouble. "Why is he there?"

It was Monday morning, and I had come into the office because I didn't want to talk to him. I hadn't really thought about what he had said about getting rich together or anything. I was sort of hoping it would just go away. I only wanted to think about my case.

"He needs a place to stay." I headed back to my desk, seeking refuge in my cup of coffee.

She turned toward me, continuing her line of questioning. "No. *Why*, as in, what is his motive for being at your place, for being in L.A.?"

"Oh, that."

"Yes, *that*," she snapped. "That which I asked you to find out about a week ago."

"Yeah."

She arched an eyebrow. "And?"

"And," I said, sitting, spinning in my chair, hoping to avoid Erika's gaze, "he wants to manage my career."

"Your career? Your acting career?"

"That's the one." Just keep spinning, just keep spinning. "He's hoping he can get me some jobs and take his percentage."

She stepped closer. "You're not an actor anymore."

"I told him that."

"Would you stop that?"

I stopped turning in my chair and looked at her. I folded my arms, looking and feeling pretty petulant.

"You're considering it, aren't you?" she said.

I shrugged. "It's complicated."

She put a hand on her hip. "*Really?*"

"You wouldn't get it. We were watching *Commando,* and I was thinking about the first time we watched it together. About how... we connected."

Erika put up a hand. "I don't know if you can trust him,

Jimmy. I don't want him to take advantage of you."

"You don't want a family member to take advantage of my newfound fame for their own financial gain. Is that what I'm hearing?"

I admit, that was a low blow I'd aimed at Erika. She had, in fact, taken advantage of my fame. True, it was to save the firm, but...

She put up a hand. "Fine. You do you, Jimmy. That's what you're going to do anyway. I'm just trying to protect you from your own dumb self." She turned and started walking out then stopped and spun back. "When you watched *Commando* that first time, I was upstairs by myself. Because that movie was gross." She turned on her heel and strode out of the office.

---

BLAKE CARROLL III was Patrick Beverly's best friend, and while he was still a student at USC, he had founded a startup tech company that was housed in Silicon Beach.

Because L.A. loves a sequel, the aptly named Silicon Beach is the hub of the tech industry here. It's close to the beach (duh) and not far from LAX, in case you need to hop on a plane to go somewhere to convince investors to give you millions of dollars for your app or website or whatever allegedly disruptive technology you're working on.

The particular stretch of Silicon Beach I was headed to was in Playa Vista. Which meant, at some point, in order to get there from the office, I had to take the most annoying highway in L.A.: the 405. It was a wide river of concrete that originated in the Valley and ribboned its way down to Orange County. On the 405, every lane is the slow lane. The 405 does not care if it's hot and your AC isn't working. It does not care if you are late for your plane. And it does not care if construction brings it down from six lanes to three — nope, two — during rush hour.

There was no other way. Unless I took surface streets, of course, but Patrick didn't have that much time.

So it was the 10 to the 405, and the B-52's "Planet Claire" that took me from Century City over to Playa Vista, one of those modern, planned neighborhoods that was supposed to be a potent mix of life, work, and play, with everything you needed within walking distance. It was built on the former grounds of Hughes Aircraft Company — you know, *the* Howard Hughes, the one Leo played in the movie where he couldn't decide which pea on his plate he could eat. Ultimately, though, Playa Vista feels more like *The Truman Show* than a real place to live. This is L.A. If we were meant to walk, why would we have cars?

I was hoping that Blake — oh, man, how did he get that name? — could shed some light on Patrick's whereabouts last week. Or, maybe if I was lucky, he might have seen something. With the clock ticking down to Friday, I was desperate for any clues I could get.

"Ghost Town" by The Specials had just come on when I entered the area's central parking garage. Up and around I went until I found a spot, parking next to an iridescent orange sedan with an airbrushed Jerry Orbach on the trunk. In L.A. everyone gets a stan.

Just outside, I found a helpful map to this prefabricated, futuristic society and made my way to Blake's office inside a shared workspace.

It was open and wide, with exposed rafters. A chalkboard — very retro — listed the names of the companies and which of the spaces they occupied that day. Each space's name was accompanied by a changeable status that described, it seems, a vibe: Chill. Grooving. Not Right Now.

Blake's company was called ... sigh... GetIt, a financial app that was supposed to beat the market and help you, wait for it, get yours. As far as I could tell from his website, none of the founders had any actual experience in financial markets. But when you know how to code...

I found him and his fellow disrupters in a vibrant, blue conference room whose vibe was listed on the chalkboard as "Winning It." Through the glass, I could see four tech bros deep in conversation. On the white board were lots of graphs and jargon I did not have the brain to understand or, actually, care about. All of them were in their early twenties and all wore the same basic uniform, untucked button-down shirts with shorts. Two were barefoot, and the other two wore sneakers without socks. I'm as SoCal as the next person, but this was taking business casual too far.

The one at the whiteboard noticed me staring at them. The other three turned their heads, and now everyone was staring at me.

I knocked on the glass as I opened the door. "I'm looking for Blake."

Two of them exchanged glances as though to say, *Which Blake?* One Blake sat at the table; the other leaned against the wall.

Of course. I pointed to the brown-haired dude against the wall. "That one."

He pushed off. A look of recognition. "Oh, right. You're that detective guy that called."

"I am. You have a minute?"

The only Blake that mattered to my case checked in with his partners who looked back at him with a bit of wide-eyed confusion. He waved off their worries as he headed toward me. "Let's grab some snacks and talk," he said as he padded by me in his bare feet and headed down the hall. I waved bye to his friends and followed.

In the break room, he grabbed a snack bag of hot, cheesy pretzels and took a fruit-flavored water from the fridge. "You want anything, it's like, it's there to grab."

An actor — even a former one — is always trained to take snacks and water when they're offered. You have no idea when you're going to get another chance at a free bag of potato chips and water. I took both.

"What's this about?" he asked, pulling open his pretzel bag.

"It's about Patrick," I said.

Blake grinned. "Patrick's great." A thought bubbled through his head and his grin disappeared. "Wait. Is he OK?"

"He is not."

A twenty-something Black guy with glasses squeezed between us, trying to get to the fridge.

I looked at Blake. "Is there someplace we can talk?"

Worried, he nodded and led me to a quiet part of the common area. A garage door was open to the world while we sat on a rock bench, surrounded by drought-tolerant plants.

"When was the last time you saw him?" I asked.

"Patrick?" Blake thought as he crunched on a pretzel. "Last week. Like, Wednesday or something. What's going on?"

I took a sip of my water. "He's been kidnapped."

"What the fuck?" he said in mid-crunch. He swallowed unchewed pieces, and I could tell it hurt. "That happens? People actually get...?"

I nodded. "Friday night he was taken by two men, just outside of his place."

"Whoa."

Whoa, indeed.

"You saw him Wednesday night?" I said.

He was thrown. "It could've been Thursday." He pulled out his phone and started scrolling. "Oh, shit." Blake looked up at me. "Thursday." He sat up. I guess I had his full attention now. "Does this mean I was the last one to see him alive?"

"Did you kidnap him?"

Blood drained from Blake's face and he licked his tongue. "What? No. No, no." He shook his head. "I was out with the bros." He pointed back towards the conference room.

He was telling the truth. "Then you weren't the last one to see him alive."

Blake looked relieved and started back in on his pretzels.

I said, "What did you do? That Thursday. Where did you see him?"

"It was at his place. There was a party. Patrick always threw the best parties."

I wiped my eyes, tried to keep from looking frustrated. I really needed Blake to stay focused.

"Anyone there that shouldn't have been?"

Blake crunched, shook his head no, but then nodded his head. "There were a couple of guys. They didn't really fit in. They were a little older. They dressed a little..."

Poorer, I was guessing. Something Blake didn't want to come out and say.

"How did they know about the party?"

Blake shrugged. "How does anyone this day and age hear about a party? People in your circle? You hear about it and you just" — another shrug — "show up. People just find out."

"What happened to them? Did they do anything weird?"

"Besides, like, not being cool?"

I shook my head, not understanding. "What do you mean, not cool?"

"They didn't talk. Mingle. Just like… watched. Not cool." He shook his head. "They didn't stay long. Patrick talked to them, though. He's super friendly. Totally cool."

"What did he say?"

Blake shook his head. "I don't know, man. There was this girl, you know?" He gave me a lopsided smile, which turned into a frown. "You think it was those guys who kidnapped Patrick?"

"Maybe? I don't know. It's possible. It'd be great if you could describe them."

Blake's face went blank. "Like I said, they were… older. Shit. Sorry, man."

At least he tried.

I leaned back and chewed on a potato chip. So I wasn't wrong. Patrick was being surveilled. Pretty ballsy on the guys to show up at a party.

"Do you know anyone else that was there that might have a better description?" I ventured.

Blake sighed. "I'll ask around."

I thanked him and asked, "What was he doing this summer?"

Blake shoved another pretzel in his mouth. "What do you mean?"

I sighed heavily. "Come on, man. Throw me a bone. Patrick told his mom he was looking into working for some charities. But we both know that was probably bullshit."

"OK, all right, you don't have to go so Veronica Mars on me. My guy just wanted to have an easy summer, OK? His dad is always on him and he wanted some cover, you know?" Blake explained.

"Cover for what?"

"For nothing." Another pretzel. "He was at home or out. He's twenty. What do you want him to do, work?"

Fair point. By the time I was twenty, I wasn't working. Sure, that could've been because I was in rehab and studios weren't really interested in trying to insure me, but…

"He's been my best friend since Saint Matthews," Blake said.

I chomped into a chip, not surprised to hear they'd attended one of the best private high schools in the city.

"He has worked *hard*. He deserved some time, you know?" He added, "Is his girlfriend OK?"

I paused mid-chew. "His girlfriend?"

"Yeah. She doesn't know yet? Oh, man." He took a drink

of his grapefruit-flavored water, and followed up it with a pretzel.

"His parents didn't tell me about her." And I hadn't really seen anyone who seemed like a girlfriend on Patrick's socials.

Blake's eyes widened. "Oh, yeah. They didn't really, you know, like her. Especially not his dad."

"No?"

His head wobbled. "She's Black. And a musician. So, you know." He leaned forward. "Patrick and his dad... Patrick would tell me about these blowout fights they would have." Blake shook his head. "Patrick would let his father have it. They did *not* see eye to eye on anything."

"Like what?"

Blake shrugged. "Family fortune stuff. Patrick's future. Blah, blah, blah, you know? You know how fathers are."

Boy, did I.

"But, money mostly. Patrick was going to stick with his own path and his Dad could not shake him from it. I was trying to get Patrick to invest in my app, but I couldn't get him to do it.

"No?"

Blake sighed. "Yeah. The thing is, this app, it's awesome." That was a little bit of a lie. Forgivable hyperbole maybe. "I kept telling Patrick that it's going to blow up when it's ready. We just need some more funding to get it over the line."

"Strange he wasn't interested in something that's totally going to blow up," I said.

"Right? But Patrick's all about the tangible. Like real world stuff. As if the internet wasn't real." I didn't want to break it to Blake, so I let him keep talking. "But that's where he wants to make his money. Companies that make stuff. Or real estate. Real 20th Century kind of shit."

Blake shook his head in confusion while I nodded. Maybe Patrick was trying to strike out on his own rather than stay in the shadow of his internet venture capitalist father.

Blake stopped shaking his head and stared at me for a second. I could see an idea crossing Blake's mind. "You should invest."

"I don't have millions of dollars."

"Oh," he said, disappointed. "But, every little bit." He turned upbeat. "It's going to be massive. One of the big guys? They'll buy us out rather than go head to head." He was breathing heavily, sounding a little bit desperate as he pronounced, "Anyone who buys in now is going to be *rich*."

Man, it was hard to turn down *that* pitch. But somehow, I managed.

# 9

—

I SAT IN my car and wondered if needing some venture capital was enough of a motive to kidnap and threaten your best friend. I shrugged off the idea. Everything about his voice and actions told me that Blake was being honest with me. More honest than the Beverlys, anyway. They conveniently left out Patrick's *girlfriend*. Blake had given me her name. Well, her stage name. Liza Borden, a mashup of one of America's most beloved singers and most of the countries most notorious singers.

Chef's kiss. No notes. She's a rock star.

Feeling like a creep, I slipped into her DMs. I wasn't sure how else to get a hold of her. As it turned out, she was a fan.

*OMG. When I as a kid, we'd watch your movies all the time*

*on DVD!* she DM'd me in reply.

That felt good. We arranged to meet in about an hour.

I checked out her music as I drove east across the city to Echo Park, the Brooklyn of L.A. Liza was a twenty-first-century Dylan-goes-electric meets Ani DiFranco, and yet totally her own thing.

If I'm being honest, I had always wanted a rock star for a girlfriend. The live shows with the screaming fans. The styles. The outrageous behavior. The whole fucking rock and roll attitude.

Of course, that fantasy ignored all the terrible parts. The touring, the endless sound checks, the terrible attitude of entitled fans, the easy access to drugs and booze to numb you out or lift you up, and an industry that sees you as a dollar sign — if you're lucky.

It was all something I recognized.

Just after lunchtime, we sat at a plastic table outside a coffeeshop on Glendale Boulevard, a big, noisy street running north and south. "She's Not Me" by Jenny Lewis could be heard coming from the open door of the place. I shook my iced coffee in its plastic cup, rattling the ice and stirring up the sugar on the bottom.

"I'm *not* his girlfriend. We broke up," she said with a bit of acid.

I guess Blake wasn't in the loop. Liza had nodded when I told her about the kidnapping, taking it in, but she didn't freak out. At least not that I could see. Maybe she was still figuring out where she stood on the subject of Patrick Beverly in their post-relationship status. It didn't sound like the relationship ended well.

"How long did you guys see each other?" I asked, slipping on my sunglasses.

"Let's not make it more than it was. We dated for like three months." She sucked on the straw of her iced latte. Liza was in her early twenties, probably twenty-three, twenty-four. She had two short pigtails and her eyes were hidden behind Ray-Bans. She wore a daisy-yellow tank top and military pants cut into shorts. Her look was finished by a pair of Doc Martens.

"How did you two meet?" I thought about getting a muffin. The potato chips at Blake's weren't a good replacement for lunch. Then again, neither was a blueberry muffin. Focus, Jimmy.

"At a club. He was trying to impress everyone. Buying round after round."

"Sounds like a monster," I said.

"It should've been a red flag. He was *too* friendly." She shrugged. "But, you know, it's kinda cool to spend without a care in the world." Liza leaned forward. "I'm not normally this shallow."

I put up a hand. "I get it. Money can be pretty intoxicating."

She paused. "Why aren't the police asking me questions?

If he's been kidnapped, shouldn't I be talking to someone official?"

"The Beverlys want to keep this quiet," I said, taking a sip of my coffee.

She shook her head, not surprised but disappointed. "It's a fucked-up family, Jimmy." She took a breath. "Patrick told me he was practically raised by nannies. They probably only want him back because of how it looks." She made a face. "His folks are going to pay the ransom, right? Whatever they're asking for?"

"If I don't find him, yeah..."

Liza shook her head. "They really should've called the FBI."

It was my turn to make a face.

"I didn't mean..."

"It's all right."

Liza nodded and swirled her drink. "Patrick's funny. Charming. It smoothes over the red flags."

That felt familiar.

"Yeah, he's younger than me, but he's seen the world, so he's not totally dumb and immature like other twenty year olds. But..." She glanced away at a passing car. "In the end, though, it wasn't like, you know, gonna last."

"Why not?"

"I started feeling like I was just a prop," Liz said, shaking her head. "He would show me off to his rich friends, to impress them how cool he was." She put her latte on the table and folded her arms. "He would take me to these dinners at *amazing* places and then once the food came, he's ignoring me and it's turned into a business pitch. Worst Spago dinner ever."

I guess he wasn't at home chilling like Blake thought and he wasn't interning like his mother believed.

"And I had always wanted to go to Spago," Liza said as she snatched her latte and sipped again.

"Me, too," I commiserated, not admitting I had been permanently banned. Wolfgang Puck disapproves when you set fire to your own dessert.

"I grew up middle class in the Valley, I didn't need his rich kid bullshit, you know?"

I nodded as I thought about the Beverlys and the conflicting stories I was getting about Patrick. I got it. I had been Rashomoned a lot in the past. But as Gordon mentored me, he would say, "It might all sound conflicting and you think someone's lying, but more often than not, there's the truth somewhere in that mess."

I cleared my throat. "What sort of business was he conducting at these dinners?"

Liza rolled her eyes behind her sunglasses. "Real estate. All the fucking time. This building, that building. This chunk of land, that chunk of land. It was all so capitalistic for my taste. After awhile, you tune it out."

"How was it going for him? He land any deals?"

She shook her head and grabbed her drink. "No," she said flatly. "He was getting desperate. I think a deal went south and he pissed some people off. He wouldn't talk about it. He started to get anxious. He was trying to hide it all from his parents. Especially his dad."

"Why?"

She shrugged. "His dad doesn't think highly of Patrick. At least, that's what he said. He wanted to prove his dad wrong, you know?"

I totally got the desire of proving a parent wrong. I chewed my lip. A business deal going wrong, pissing off the wrong people, that could certainly be a strong motive to kidnap someone.

"You wouldn't happen to know who he was meeting with, do you?" I took a sip of my now watered down iced coffee.

"They were all dudes in suits, Jimmy." She paused. "Wait. There was one guy. He was totally familiar."

I shifted in my seat as she tried to think of his name. I just needed one name.

"And I saw him again. Like three weeks ago." She pointed down the street. "I remember because I was playing a gig one night and before the show one of the dudes in suits like tries to fight Patrick." She paused. "Not *fight* fight. It was all just trash talk. But this guy was pissed. *And* he brought back up. A light skinned Black guy. Brother was built. Looked hot in his suit. The bouncers broke it up before anything got serious."

Two guys. Could be the two from the party Blake mentioned.

"Patrick didn't get tossed because he was with me. He was pretty rattled."

"It'd be great if you could remember a name."

Something caught her attention. Liza Borden pointed across the street. "There he is."

I looked over. A city bus hissed to a stop. The doors slid open and passengers stepped off as others waited to get on.

"Where?" I said.

"There," she emphasized. "On the side of the bus."

Plastered on the bus was an advertisement. A man in his late forties with tousled shoulder-length black hair, like a warrior, stared out of the bus. Even I knew the guy. I had seen his dumb face all over LA. He was an ambulance-chasing lawyer named Derrick Sayles.

# 10
—

THE BEVERLYS LIVED over in the Pacific Palisades, a hop, skip, and a jump from the beaches. Beverly Hills would be too gauche for such billionaires, I supposed and Malibu would be too obvious.

The Palisades was a refuge. Hilly and leafy green, which in a desert basin like L.A., with its water restrictions, seemed impossible and possibly wrong.

On the way up to their house, I passed through the Village, the walkable, downtown area of the neighborhood. You know you're there when you start spotting older ladies in wide-brimmed hats. This is not to be confused with the Palisades Village, which is *in* the Village, but is an outdoor shopping area.

The Beverlys' home was modest for billionaires, but maybe that's just my own expectations of how a billionaire should spend their money on housing. While it was big, it wasn't sprawling. It was a mansion of good taste, if there was such a thing. From the road, you could see the two stories and the glass foyer occupying both. I had called ahead, so at the gate, I was waved in by the guard without so much as a "Hello, how are you, sir?"

An actual, real-life butler opened the door. He wore a crisp, white shirt to go with his even crisper white pants. He nodded and told me to follow him through the house, which was a throwback to a very different time and place. Antiques vases, lamps, and statues sat on cabinets and credenzas that could've been pulled from Marie Antoinette's boudoir. English landscapes by Old Masters you've never heard of hung on the walls. The place didn't feel old, though. Just plain, old-fashioned opulence.

The butler brought me out back to the poolside, which was large, shimmering, and emerald.

So this was where all the money went. Beyond the pool was The View. There are certain places in L.A. where you will literally have your breath stolen from you when you look out, and this was one of them. The deep blue ocean stretched to infinity. I could see the rest of the Palisades and Santa Monica to the south, as well as Topanga and the road to Malibu to the north.

It was a view you could fall into forever.

"Mr. Cooper."

I tore my eyeballs away.

Eva Beverly was there, seated under a patio table's umbrella, drinking iced tea in a sundress.

As I strolled closer to her, I glimpsed documents on the table in front of her. I assumed they were from the family's nonprofit she now oversaw.

"Please, call me Jimmy," I said, taking the chair across from her as she set the paperwork aside. "Beautiful place." Which is an understatement she probably heard a million times before.

"Thank you." She had heard it a million times.

"Where's the mister?"

"He'll be home soon. Work."

"And I thought being rich meant you never had to work."

Her jaw tightened as she tried to smile off my comment. I had stepped into something. She said, "There are a lot of people that work for us. People who rely on us to show up. Any sort of hint of something going wrong could cause... Fortunes have been lost just by rumor."

I nodded. The butler placed a glass of water to my right and asked if I wanted anything else. I shook my head, and he disappeared in the soundless way that butlers do.

"Sounds terrible, having all of those dependents. Still," I said, picking up the glass, "I'd rather have a billion dollars in the bank than nothing."

She looked at me, her eyes soft around the edges. "Money doesn't protect you from tragedy, Jimmy." Her voice almost wasn't there.

I winced at my flippant remark; I had lost track of my audience. I shook my head by way of apology.

She said nothing. "You had something?" she prompted.

Right. That's why I was here. I nodded and took out my phone, then showed her the picture I took of the bus. "Do you know that man?" I asked.

She took the phone with one hand and grabbed her tea with the other. Her nails were freshly manicured in a deep maroon. They shone and curved and could probably cut through steel. Eva Beverly flushed.

"Yes. I know Derrick Sayles. Does he have something to do with Patrick?" She handed my phone back.

"Possibly. It looks like Sayles and your son were working together. On some deal."

Eva shook her head. "You must be mistaken. Sayles was briefly a business parter of my *husband*."

I frowned. I was pretty sure Liza Borden wouldn't confuse Patrick and Robert Beverly. "What happened?" I said.

She huffed, impatient.

Another voice answered. "He wanted to move up in the world."

I turned to see Robert Beverly striding towards us, rolling

up the sleeves of his pale blue shirt and handing off his suit coat to the butler as he came. I checked my watch. 3:30. Sure, that could be the end of the workday.

Robert leaned down and kissed his wife, then sat next to her. He took a breath and said, "Sayles is trying to leverage his way of the practice of law. He doesn't want to always be known as an ambulance chaser."

Mom used to trash-talk lawyers like Sayles, whose slogan was "Who do you want to sue?" She hated their gaudy ads, their tactics, and how they would take sizable chunks of the client's monetary award because they worked on contingency. "Those lawyers give real lawyers a bad name," she would say. Never mind that they were real lawyers with real law degrees and that maybe it was the system that was terrible.

Robert continued, "It turns out it wasn't just us he approached with his opportunities." The way he said the word, he wasn't impressed. "He's been making overtures to startups, entertainment, all kinds of things, including moving into the nonprofit scene." I glanced over at Eva. What little she revealed told me Sayles wasn't particularly welcome in the nonprofit world. "He was hoping to secure some social capital as well."

"What happened?"

"I took a look at some of his proposals. Some were interesting. But he didn't actually have any capital of his own. He's rather cash poor. He's overextended himself into other real estate projects and expected us to fund his ideas. They were great ideas, it isn't our fault he didn't have the money. Why are you asking?"

"He thinks Derrick has Patrick," snapped Eva.

"What?" Robert looked at me, anxious.

I put up my hands. "That's not what I said. I said that Patrick and Derrick were working on a deal and things may have gone wrong. That could be a motive. Especially if Derrick is overextended as you say."

He shook his head. "Patrick wasn't working on a deal with anyone."

"His girlfriend disagrees."

Robert turned to me, his jaw tight. "The... *musician*."

I knew what he meant.

"She told me — " I started.

"It's not true," said Robert, getting angry.

"Mr. Beverly — "

He put up a hand and I shut up. "My son Patrick isn't involved in any sort of business deals. He doesn't have the head for it. He's a twenty year old who has never had to work a day in his life."

"Maybe he's trying to show you he's more capable than you think."

Robert snorted at the idea. "I don't know what this girl thinks she saw, but it wasn't *my son* doing any sort of deal."

"Right now, it's what I got," I said.

"It's 'what you got'?" he barked. He looked at his wife and then back to me. "When we hired you, we expected you to deliver, Mr. Cooper. This doesn't feel like delivering."

"It's only been a day, Mr. Beverly. I think you need to recalibrate your expectations." Wow, I sounded all professional and boundary-drawing. Gordon Bixby would be proud.

Without looking at him, Eva said, "He's doing his best."

"It's not good enough." He glared at me. "I need an ass-kicker. Are you an ass-kicker, Mr. Cooper?"

Spoilers: I was not.

I'm not sure who he thought he had hired. I leaned back and really looked at him, and I saw it. A man who all his life never wanted for anything. Everything he could've wanted was his. Now here he was, confronting a situation where his wealth couldn't change the outcome. He was powerless. And he didn't like it.

"I want to assure you, Mr. Beverly, I'm doing my job. Whoever took your son, they planned this, and that means we have to play catch-up." He shifted in his seat, unpersuaded. "You're free to let me go, of course."

Eva put her hand up before her husband could agree with my resignation bluff. "No one is letting anyone go." She turned to her husband. "Time is important. We stick with Jimmy."

Robert Beverly stood up and walked into the house.

After a moment, she said to me, "Don't worry about him. His bark can be worse than his bite."

Can be? That wasn't encouraging.

# 11

—

I HAD A PRIME suspect. Or at least, *a* suspect.

It was Tuesday afternoon when I parked near the law offices of Derrick Sayles on Wilshire in the Miracle Mile area. As is typical for L.A., the area feels like it's in a constant state of renewal: a new art museum, new office buildings, new restaurants. The only thing that hadn't changed was the tar pits, and that was because they were a tourist destination. But I'm sure there was a developer out there who was thinking, *Why tar? Why not a mixed-use office/shopping complex?*

When I got home the night before and Dad wasn't there, I had breathed a sigh of relief. Maybe he changed his mind and had gone back home. That would mean I didn't have to be a better person.

Twenty minutes after my lamb biryani arrived from my favorite Indian place, though, he showed up. I could smell on his breath that he had had a couple. He wasn't drunk, but he was definitely in a "good mood." He wouldn't tell me who he had been hanging out with; he just wagged a finger at my questions and said that "all would be revealed in time." Then he pointed at my food and asked if he could have some.

It was a real pleasure watching him struggle through the Indian food.

Instead of talking, we watched a double feature. *Rambo: First Blood Part II* followed by *Rambo III*. After that, it was awkward and weird. We talked about the movies but we completely avoided talking about where he had been. It was easier to pretend like everything was normal and I could enjoy having my dad back. After the movies, we said good night and retreated to our corners of my place.

After parking near the tar pits and feeding the meter, I entered the taupe-colored lobby of the building where Sayles kept his office, which really spoke to the whole vibe of the place. Built in the early eighties — and I was surprised it hadn't been replaced yet — it came off as peak mediocrity. No one working here was at the top of their field. The dentist in the building, I bet he was fine, but he wasn't going to be the best dentist in L.A. Sure, he could fill your cavity, but isn't that required to even be a dentist?

I'm sure he could fill a cavity as good as the next guy, but isn't that damning with faint praise?

Sayles's office was on the third floor and right off the elevator, just behind the dark brown eight-foot-high double doors, chosen, I'm sure, for maximum impression. But then, once you've seen one massive door, haven't you seen them all? I knew I was being a snob, but I didn't care. For all my mother's exactitude, she did know how to create a work environment that was classy and impressive.

Inside the reception area, it was a little better. Sayles had laid down the cash for nice leather seats that ringed the space. A couple sat in two of them, holding hands and whispering together. The man had gauze over his left eye and bruises on his face. Across from them was a man in sunglasses and a baseball hat pulled low. He hugged himself and looked down at the floor.

I approached the receptionist, sitting behind a chest-high counter. She looked to be in her sixties, thick and squat with deeply tanned skin. Her light-brown hair was formerly blonde. She looked up to me with watery eyes. "You don't look injured," she said in a Long Island gravel, followed by labored breathing.

"Only my heart," I simpered.

She raised annoyed and thinly plucked eyebrows. "Excuse me?"

Now that I had her on the ropes, I went in for the kill. "I'm here to see Derrick Sayles." I punctuated my ask with a cute half-smile.

Her eyebrows lowered, and she turned to her computer screen. "Do you have an appointment?"

Did she not see my *smile*? Maybe I should pay a visit to the mediocre dentist on my way out.

"I don't." This time, I went full smile. "Do I need one?"

Her eyes met mine. "Mr. Sayles is a very busy man."

"Of course. I would expect Mr. Sayles to be busy. After all, he's got all those billboards."

She was not impressed. "So you *don't* have an appointment?"

Defeated, I admitted, "No. No, I do not."

"He's not seeing people without an appointment."

"Like, never?"

She leaned back and shook her head slowly. She was not succumbing to my charms. The direct approach it was.

"I'll wait," I said and turned toward the seats.

She repeated to my back, "He won't see you without an appointment."

I turned around. "Well, when's the next available appointment?"

She peeked at her screen. "Two weeks."

"Two weeks?" I gawked. "You didn't even search."

She said nothing.

"This involves a case. A case that I'm working on and that Mr. Sayles might be involved in."

The receptionist scowled. "Are you a lawyer?" Her voice was filled with suspicion.

"I'm a private detective."

Her face squished like she had tasted something rotten, and I heard a creak as one of the waiting clients shifted in their chair. I really wished there had been some sort of soothing Muzak to cover this whole uncomfortable moment.

"I'll just wait."

"You can do that," she said, "but he's not going to — "

"Yes, see me. Got it." I took a pen and one of Sayles's business cards and wrote on the back. I handed her the card. "This is who I'm representing. When he wants to see me, I'll be over there." I pointed to an empty chair near the couple.

She reluctantly took the card, and I sat close to the couple. I watched as the receptionist looked at the card and then back at me. I could see the gears turning in her head. She recognized the Beverlys' name and was trying to decide what to do. Finally, she lifted her phone, pushed a button and turned away as she whispered into the receiver.

By the look on her face, I didn't think I was going to get in that way. Time to take another approach. I leaned toward the couple. "Hey there."

They eyed me — OK, she eyed me, he only had one eye to give.

"Hi," the woman replied softly.

"Did it hurt?" I asked the man.

"Oh, yeah." His voice was deep. "Almost lost the eye."

"Bastards," I said, not knowing anything about the case. But then, here he was, I'm sure, planning on suing someone. And knowing Sayles, he wasn't going to settle for what would make this man whole and some pain and suffering. Derrick was going to try and get them into another tax bracket, and for a good sized fee. I nodded sympathetically. "I was wondering if we could switch?"

"Switch?" asked the woman.

"Yeah, I really need to see Mr. Sayles. It's kind of time sensitive," I chuckled, trying to make my request seem totally normal and not weird at all. "So, I'm wondering if we could switch appointments."

The guy looked at the woman. She shook her head, saying, "We can't wait two weeks."

I leaned closer and confidentially said, "It's not going to be two weeks." I shook my head toward the receptionist. "She's saying that to get rid of me. You two have a case; I'm sure of it."

"I don't think so," the woman replied.

"OK, how about this? My *mom* is a lawyer. A really good one. She could see you immediately."

"But... we're here now," the guy rumbled.

"We're good," the woman said with finality.

I took the hint and looked across the way at the other guy waiting. He turned his head and body away from me, like he was trying to be invisible. The receptionist had put her phone back on the receiver and was watching me carefully.

"Any word?" I asked.

She said nothing.

I crossed reception and plunked down next to the guy who didn't want to be seen. "What brings you here, friend?" I pointed to the guy with the patch over his eye. "I know why he's here. Who do you want to sue?" I leaned forward, trying to catch the eyes of my new friend, but I couldn't see past the sunglasses.

Then I took a breath. "Matty?" I whispered.

He looked at me. Holy shit. It *was* Matty. Matty Goodman, L.A.'s newest boy detective. I was about to shout it to the waiting room when he put his hand on my arm and shushed me. We both considered the receptionist, but she was on a call.

"What are you *doing* here?" I asked.

"I'm working a case."

I cocked my head. Had I heard him right?

He shifted toward me and repeated himself. "I'm working a *case*."

"That's so weird. So am I."

"Yeah, I know. I heard you announce it to everyone in the room." He shook his head like *he* was the one dealing with an amateur.

"Who are you working for?"

"Who are *you* working for?" he retorted.

I crossed my arms. "Listen, I don't need you fucking up my case with whatever dumb case you have going on."

"My case isn't dumb, Jimmy."

I put up a hand. "Whatever. I'm just... I have a time-sensitive one."

"Aren't they *all* time-sensitive?" he replied.

Matty had a good point, but I wasn't going to tell him that. "Some more than others."

A voice called out. "Peter Ostrum?"

I looked at Matty as he stood. "Jesus Christ, Matty." Peter Ostrum had played Charlie in *Willy Wonka and the Chocolate Factory*. I grabbed his arm before he got too far. "I really need to see Sayles. How can we make this work?"

"You come up with some ideas, we'll workshop them after... my appointment." He smirked as he walked across the reception and shook hands with a young woman I assumed was Mr. Sayles's assistant. As she led him away, Matty waved back at me.

Waved. Back. At. Me.

The nerve. The gall.

And then I had to ask myself, what case was Matty working on? It couldn't possibly be...

I grunted "Fuck" at the thought.

The receptionist gave me the stink eye. And yeah, I wasn't going to see her boss without an appointment. I stood up, cutting my losses, and left.

There were other ways to see Derrick Sayles.

# 12

—

EVA BEVERLY ANSWERED on the second ring. "Mr. Cooper, any news?" I could hear the strain in her voice.

She was never going to call me Jimmy. I was back in my car, rubbing my forehead. "No, nothing yet." Time to get to the point. "Did you and your husband hire another detective?"

A long silence on the other end was pretty much all the answer I needed, but she felt like explaining herself.

"Yes," Eva admitted. "We thought... well, after last night, Robert and I discussed it. We thought it would be good to have more than one person looking for our son."

I stopped rubbing my forehead and started squeezing my eyes. "It would've been nice to know, Mrs. Beverly. As a bit of professional courtesy."

"Yes, I see that now."

That was the only apology I was going to get. I pressed forward. "But, Matty Goodman?" I could think of half a dozen more qualified private investigators. Or, you know, going to the cops.

She sighed. "Edward recommended him."

Edward? Again? What was up with this guy? Did he not *know* about Matty's staggering lack of experience?

"Mrs. Beverly, I have some concerns about hiring Matty Goodman."

"This wouldn't be professional jealousy, would it?"

I gritted my teeth to prevent a scream. Because it wasn't. It really wasn't. Was it?

"Mrs. Beverly, it *isn't* — "

She cut me off. "Time is of the essence. And, quite frankly, it shouldn't matter to you how we spend our money in *our* crisis. You have a job to do, and as I recall, we're not paying you to sit on the phone and complain."

Right. They weren't.

"Just to be clear, I'm not complaining." I totally was. "I just don't want a situation where we are stepping on each other's toes."

"I guess that's up to you two." She hung up.

I stewed for a bit before realizing there wasn't much I could do at that moment. I still needed to talk to Sayles so I moved my car and found a spot where I could see the building's parking garage. I checked my watch. Three o'clock. I settled into the driver's seat and started playing Dolly's "Here You Come Again" as perhaps a prayer to the surveillance gods. Sooner or later the guy would have to leave, and I bet he didn't take public transportation home.

Everything I learned about surveillance, I learned from Gordon Bixby. He would tell me, "There's nothing *fun* about surveillance. It's time-consuming. It's boring. And you can't be distracted because the moment you check your phone... your target? He's gone." Let's all take a moment and roll our eyes at the incredibly serious use of the word "target." He was right, though. Thus the need for a never-ending playlist or I'd go crazy.

An hour or so later, my phone dinged with a text. I picked it up out of the cup holder, looking at it.

*Hey, you.*

It was from Ito.

*Hey* I typed back. *What's going on?* Smooth, Jimmy. Real smooth.

*We still good for coffee?* she replied.

Shit, shit. The coffee date. I'd said mid-week and here we were, on the cusp of mid-week.

*Yeah, yeah, coffee. Great!*

What was I doing? I didn't have time. I was in the middle of a case. A case that she can't know about.

*There's a place on Larchmont I like*, she suggested.

Larchmont was a quaint neighborhood a few blocks long and just south of Paramount. Cute shops and places to eat lined the avenue. It's a fun spot.

*Sounds great. Text me the place. What time?* I texted before realizing I was committing myself to seeing the woman I really should've been avoiding at this point.

Ito replied immediately. *I got some time around two.*

*See you tomorrow*, I typed and tossed the phone back on the passenger seat with a grunt. Shungudzo's "It's a good day (to fight the system)" started up. I ran through how to handle my coffee date with Violet Ito. She was a detective and trained to seek out the truth. I'm screwed.

But then, I wasn't doing anything *illegal*. I was doing my job. A job that she knows that I have. So everything should be just fine.

Spoilers: I didn't really believe that.

Two hours later, a black SUV pulled out of the garage, being driven by the guy that was with Sayles at the club. He paused to look both ways.

Guessing that Sayles was in the back, I started my car as the SUV turned left onto Wilshire. He was a few cars ahead of me, but I made it through the light. We went west on Wilshire, then turned south onto Fairfax Avenue, passing LACMA and the spaceship with its red swooshes that was the Petersen Car Museum. The SUV made its way up the ramp onto the 10 West just as the Dave Brubeck Quartet's "Take Five" started.

I let them get a bit ahead of me. After all, Sayles's bodyguard might have been on the lookout for tails. The only danger for me was all the other black SUVs driving around on the 10. Seriously, what is it with black SUVs in this town?

As I followed them, I deliberated on Matty working the case. It really got under my skin. I shook my head, feeling stupid. This was the same sort of bullshit I had experienced when I was an actor, when I wouldn't get a job and some other kid would. It had even irked me when I heard more about another actor and wondered why people weren't talking about *me* instead.

Mrs. Beverly wasn't wrong. She and her husband had wanted more eyes on the case, and I should chill the fuck out.

But I didn't *want* to chill out. There was something bothering me about the whole thing that I couldn't figure out. I just knew in my gut it was wrong to hire Matty Goodman. Which also begged the question: Was there someone else, or were we two idiots the only ones?

In my self-pity, I almost missed the SUV moving into the far left lane to avoid a slowdown, thanks to all that pesky merging and exiting.

"Shit."

Moving into the lane, I squeezed in front of a minivan. I waved an apology behind me, and the mom at the wheel gave me the finger.

I turned the volume up and my attention back to the case. Derrick Sayles. If he was overextended like the Beverlys said, and *if* Patrick had screwed him over... That's a lot of motive. It's money, it's personal. But even if those ifs were true...

It's one thing to want to kidnap someone but entirely another to go through with it. A kidnapping takes planning and, more importantly, willingness. Most people don't actually do bad things. It's a big leap from saying you want to do a bad thing to actually going through with it.

We crossed over the 405, and the SUV started snaking its way across, getting ready to exit. Finally, it took Centinela Avenue North, heading toward beautiful downtown Santa Monica.

Santa Monica is what TV wishes Los Angeles was, with its clean streets, walkable neighborhoods, and proximity to the beach. It's like a suburb with an ocean view.

Of course, all that beauty comes at a price. Not just the real estate prices — those too — but also the police using a heavier-than-needed hand to keep out the people they didn't think belonged.

The SUV turned off Centinela onto a side street and then made another turn. It eventually slowed and stopped in front of an apartment building.

I slid into a spot nearby, hoping to figure out what he was doing here.

The bodyguard stepped out and opened the back passenger-side door. Derrick Sayles hopped out, slipping on sunglasses. His dark hair, with a dash of white, fell to his neck, capturing a certain rock and roll vibe that made him a bit of a bad boy lawyer. It was a great brand, I had to admit. He wore a gray suit; his tie was gone, and the white button-down was unbuttoned a few extra. I wondered if he'd gotten that move from Robert Beverly. Always dress for who you want to be, not who you are.

He headed to the front of the building, where he met...

"Matty," I growled.

I got out of my car. What the hell was he doing? He was going to fuck up my stakeout.

I moved quickly down the sidewalk. I could see the two of them shaking hands and smiling at each other. Matty pointed to the building but then spotted me. His eyes went wide.

"Derrick!" I called.

As he turned, the bodyguard stepped in front of him. When you're an accident lawyer, maybe random attacks from strangers are a thing.

Matty's mouth became a thin line. His eyes burned into me.

Derrick spoke from behind his bodyguard. "Do I know

you?"

That hurt. I had been getting attention all over for just being me. "I know *you*," I said and offered him my hand.

Derrick didn't take it, and the bodyguard didn't move. Awkward. I pulled the hand back. "I don't know if you got my note..."

Matty said to me, "Sir — "

Sir? What a way to stay in character, jerk.

"Sir," he said, "we're in an important meeting. Maybe you should call Mr. Sayles's office. Make an appointment. I'm sure you could snag one in a few weeks."

I grinned. "*Or* I could talk to Mr. Sayles now."

"Mr. Sayles is *busy*," Matty replied.

Derrick looked back and forth between Matty and me. "Do you guys know each other?"

Matty shook his head no.

I said, "My name is — "

"Jimmy Cooper," finished Sayles. He put out his hand, and his bodyguard stepped away. "I read the news. Yeah, I got your note." He smiled in that noncommittal way lawyers practice in the mirror. "Sorry I couldn't see you. I had business to attend to." He nodded at the building. "So. You're representing the Beverlys."

He wasn't impressed.

"That's right."

"Funny to run into you here in Santa Monica," he said.

Matty grunted.

"Well, you know," I said brightly. "It's a small town."

"You live in Santa Monica?" asked Sayles.

"Oh. No. I mean, you know, the greater... L.A. area. The whole..." I didn't bother to finish. I turned to Matty and offered a hand. "Jimmy Cooper." If he was going to stay in character...

"Oh yeah," Matty deadpanned. "I remember you. Weren't you in those awful teen movies?"

"I was. But at least I wasn't stuck doing awful teen TV, am I right?"

I laughed. Matty did not.

Pressing on with Sayles, I asked, "Have you seen Patrick lately?"

"Patrick?" Derrick replied. Was that surprise or confusion?

"Patrick Beverly," I clarified.

Derrick's eyes narrowed. "Is there a problem?"

"Well, he's missing. More specifically, he's been kidnapped."

Matty looked like he was about to blow a gasket.

Derrick nodded and said nothing. Maybe he wasn't such a terrible lawyer after all. He was smart enough to keep his mouth shut.

I kept going. "Have you seen him since that time you and your bodyguard got tossed from the club? That must've been embarrassing."

The bodyguard took a little step toward me. Matty took a step back.

Matty grunted. "Mr. Sayles isn't here to answer questions — "

"Maybe he would if you give him a chance, person-I-just-met," I said over my shoulder. Turning back, I continued, "Given the circumstance, I think it'd be great if you started talking, Derrick."

"Is that a threat, Mr. Cooper?"

"Man, why does *everyone* call me Mr. Cooper? Jimmy. Call me Jimmy. It's so much friendlier." I looked from person to person, hoping to get it through. Turning back to Sayles, I said, "It's not a threat as in, 'Ooh, I'm going to beat you up.' It's more of an ask. Because, like, you know, we don't want things going sideways."

"*Jimmy*," started Derrick Sayles, "Yes. Patrick and I had some... words. As I'm sure you're aware, he owes me a great deal of money."

Now I was.

"Since he had not been responding to my polite requests for repayment, I went to him. I haven't seen him since." He wasn't lying. Then again, just because he might not have seen Patrick, it didn't mean other people in his employ hadn't.

"Must be a lot of money," I said, crossing my arms. "To go through all of that."

"I see what you're trying to do," said Derrick, smirking. "It's a nice suggestion. That I have a motive for hurting Patrick."

"Is he hurt? I just said he was missing."

Derrick nodded. "I don't know. But I do know I'm not the *only* one Patrick owes money. Some of them are really bad people." Derrick leaned closer. "He's quite the idiot."

With something like *that*, I had a million follow-up questions, but a woman's voice interrupted everything.

"Hey, Matty!" It was kind and friendly and belonged to a tall blonde woman who had stepped out of the apartment building. She was dressed in a T-shirt and shorts, ready for a run, about to push in some earbuds.

Matty stared at her.

She spotted me and gasped. "Oh, my God! Jimmy Cooper! I *love* you!" She looked back and forth. "Wait. Do you guys know each other?"

Sayles looked to Matty. "*Do* you guys know each other?"

The woman continued. "It's, like, a club or something? Like child actors all know each other?" She pulled her phone out of her running armband. "I gotta get a pic."

"Hold up," I said, as a few puzzle pieces fell into place, then turned to Matty. "Were you trying to sell him *your* apartment building?"

Sayles pointed at the building. "This *is* your building, right? Like *yours* yours? As in, you own the whole thing and you can sell it?"

Matty was sweating. "Yeah."

It wasn't. Matty was lying. Why he was lying I didn't know and things were moving too fast to ask.

The woman gestured to Matty and me. "Can you guys move closer together?" She held the phone at arm's length, leaned in next to me, and snapped a pic. "My friends are going to freak! Bye, Matty!" And she was off on her run.

"Who the *fuck* is Matty?"asked Derrick. "Are you Matty? Are you just some actor?"

Matty wasn't talking so much as hemming and hawing. When the bodyguard decided to get involved and stepped closer to him, he crumbled like a fistful of crackers.

"Hey, hey, OK, OK!" He held up his hands. "Yeah, yeah, my name is Matty Goodman. I'm a private investigator!"

The bodyguard grabbed Matty by the shirt, pulling him up and closer. Matty went pale and started breathing hard. He was scared.

"Derrick," I said, trying to sound tough.

He looked at me. Pissed. "*What*?"

"Listen, we're just trying to find out what happened to Patrick."

"Oh, so you're working *together*."

Shit. "I can see how it looks that way. But we're not — "

He wasn't listening. "We're done. Let's go, Richard."

Richard — the bodyguard — dropped Matty, who fell on

his ass.

Derrick opened his car door. "If I ever see you again, I will be filing a restraining order."

# 13

——

"YOU OK?" I asked Matty, who sat on the grass, right where he had been dropped by the bodyguard, arms on his knees. He was pale and breathing fast, and I thought he might throw up. So, no, he wasn't OK. But this was how polite society behaved. We always ask someone who is clearly not OK if they are OK, like we're trying to avoid really getting involved.

He nodded, avoiding my eyes.

"This business, it can turn aggressive pretty quick," I said.

"*I'm all right.*"

"Yeah, you said."

"God, you couldn't just, like... let me do this thing." He was pissed. "I had a *plan*." Which probably didn't include getting assaulted. "And then you come along and you fuck it up."

"I didn't mean to."

He shook his head. "That's a lie."

It was.

"OK. I didn't come here with the *plan* of ruining whatever it was you were up to, but..." I paused, ready to lay it out there. "It turns out we're on the same case."

Matty rolled his eyes. "No shit, Sherlock."

"You knew?"

"Of course I knew. The Beverlys told me when they hired me."

Embarrassed and weak in the knees, I sat next to him on the ground, looking out at the street.

Matty went on. "They got me up to speed, told me what they knew — "

I bit my lip. That was how he had ended up at Derrick's office so quickly.

"And I took it from there." He was getting his color back. A couple of deep breaths. "He's heavily invested in real estate all over Los Angeles County. Most of it in shit apartment buildings in shit neighborhoods." He looked at me. "It was all he could afford."

"He's stuck with bad investments."

"I was hoping I could get him interested in this place." He tipped his head back at the apartment building. "Build some trust, develop a lead. If he's holding Patrick, maybe he's holding him at one of his properties."

"Wow, Matty," I said, stunned. "That's... actually good."

I am not crafty like that.

He didn't know how to reply to the compliment, so he muttered, "Thanks."

Maybe he would make a good private detective, but I wasn't going to tell him that. I looked at the building. It was a nice place. "*Do* you own the place?"

Matty burst out laughing. "Most of my money got conned out of me by my business manager. I do have a corner apartment on the front. I'm lucky I can afford the rent."

"It is Santa Monica."

He agreed, and we sat in silence for a beat.

"I am sorry," I said. "About..." I pointed to where Sayles's car had sat.

Matty shrugged, making it very unclear if he was accepting my apology or not. I guess I really needed to go there.

"And for being an asshole the other night," I added. "I didn't... it wasn't about jealousy. At least, I don't think it was. Maybe it was a little bit about jealousy. This is — *was* — my thing, you know? But, also, like, this is a dangerous gig. You can't just jump into it."

"I'll be ready next time." There was an eerie calm to the way he said that, which worried me.

"Sure," I said. "It's... I guess I was trying to look out for you."

"I don't need you looking out for me."

I paused, realizing my apology was going to lead to another argument. "You're right," I said instead. "You're totally right." I pushed myself up off the ground and opened my arms. "Come on, bring it in."

He looked me up and down. "I'm not hugging you."

"I think you should hug me. We just made a breakthrough in our relationship."

"I don't want to hug you," he said.

"Not even a little bit?"

He said nothing.

"Look," I said, putting my arms down. "We should to work together." I offered a hand to help him up.

Matty slapped it away. "I'm not an old man," he said as he got onto his feet. "Work together? Like a buddy comedy?"

Both of us made a face. We were on the same wavelength. This wasn't going to be a buddy comedy.

"Think more of it as a collaboration," I suggested. "It doesn't have to be a competition. We share information and resources. There's a life at stake."

He crossed his arms. "Yeah, I know what's at stake."

Clearly it was going to be difficult between Matty and me. And that was OK. I was a professional, and I was going to give him the benefit of the doubt. I assumed he was as well. Besides, I had worked with some really terrible costars who will go nameless. All I'll say is it was worse than the rumors around Hoffman and Streep during *Kramer vs. Kramer.*

"Fine," he said. "We can work together. But this about Patrick. You're still an asshole."

And maybe I was. But I was happy to have the help. Time was running out.

I asked Matty, "What do you think about Sayles? You think he has Patrick?"

"Kidnapping feels personal, you know?" He was fine now, totally back to being himself. But I could see a bit of fire in his eyes that hadn't been there before. "You don't kidnap anyone anymore to make a buck. It's easier to hack a company and hold the server hostage," said Matty. "Whoever took him wants the money and a little bit of revenge. So why not Sayles? He's been screwed by the Beverlys before. Maybe this time he took it personally."

"I was thinking the same thing," I replied. "There's just something about this case that gets me."

"What's that?"

"I don't *know.*" I scratched my cheek. "There's a nagging thought. Like, why are *we* on this case? Pardon me for saying it, but you lack a certain amount of experience — "

"Fuck you," he said plainly.

"Noted. And I'm *me.* They came to me. There's lots of private investigators in this city. Why me?"

"Edward Stratton recommended me."

"And me."

I suddenly had the urge to talk to Stratton again. But I wasn't done. "And then there's Patrick."

Matty frowned, curious.

"His mom thinks he's this loving son. His best friend said he argued with his father all the time. And his girlfriend, ex-girlfriend — "

Matty stepped closer, confused. "They never mentioned a girlfriend."

"Ex. They don't like her, but *yeah*... So, I don't know. It's just... I'm bugged and I hate being bugged."

"So, what then?"

I thought about that.

"Let's stick with Sayles," I said. "He was my best lead and he has a motive."

Matty shook his head. "Is he the type, though? To do this?"

"I've been wondering that too." I looked in the direction of the departed black SUV. "Maybe he would be, with the right people." I pulled out my phone. "In the meantime, let's keep up with your idea that Patrick is being held at one of the properties Sayles owns." I called Nora.

She answered, crisp, bright, efficient. "Jimmy Cooper's office."

I tried my British accent, a bit Michael Caine with a dash of Dick Van Dyke, in an attempt to throw her off her game.

"'Allo, luv, I was hoping to speak with Mr. Cooper. Is he in?"

Matty made a sour face, and I grinned in return.

"Mr. Cooper, we've gone over this," my long-suffering assistant said. "I have caller ID."

She was unshakable. "Nora, I was wondering if we could get a list of all the properties that Derrick Says owns."

She paused. "It will take some time to go through city records — "

"And the county. He owns places all over."

Another pause. "It will take a little longer, but I can get you a list."

I thanked her and hung up. I said to Matty, "I'll get you the list as soon as I have it. You can start checking them out. Maybe start with the places within the city. Like, I doubt he's up in Palmdale."

He nodded his chin at me. "What about you?"

"I have an idea who might be a willing partner for Sayles. I just don't know his name yet."

# 14

—

TIM CURRY BELTED "I'm Going Home" while I lounged on my couch, alone. I didn't know where my dad was, and I kept pushing the mounting worry away that question caused. Instead, I focused on Patrick.

I had already found who I was looking for. It had taken me thirty minutes to put a name to Sayles's bodyguard. His name was Richard Johnson. Ricky to his friends — he couldn't exactly walk around being called Dick Johnson.

Turns out Ricky was a former Marine who had been discharged under Other Than Honorable conditions. Now, that didn't mean he was a criminal or that he had done anything wrong, but he had done something not very *right* to get that sort of dismissal from the military.

The important thing: Ricky might have been the willing participant who could turn Derrick's idea into reality. He would have the skills and the mindset to snatch a twenty-year-old like Patrick right off his stoop. And splitting $25 million could be a hell of a motivator.

I texted Blake pictures of Derrick and Ricky to see if they were the two men he had seen at Patrick's party. If he said yes, then we were really onto something. After staring at my phone for a while — why wasn't he texting me back? — I gave up and got off the couch to make some coffee. I groaned as the coffee drizzled into the glass carafe.

It wasn't about the coffee: it was about the waiting. It's a frustrating aspect of this job, the part that truly eats at me. Waiting for someone *else* to come through with information. Waiting for someone *else* to do something. All of these moments are cut out of movies and TV shows. Why? Because they're boring.

"After a lifetime of seeing some shit, I like the boring parts," Gordon Bixby would tell me as we sat, bored out of our minds in the parking lot of a motel where this married guy liked to meet his favorite sex workers. "It's nice to just sit and enjoy that I'm still walking and breathing, you know?"

I did not. And I still don't. It's what makes being a private detective the worst job ever. As I tried to warn Matty.

Though, yes, if I took a step back, I would probably realize that it's the same for everyone in every job. OK, maybe not Buddhist Monks.

I get worried, though, because of the lizard in my brain.

Metaphorically speaking.

When I get bored, especially late at night, the lizard starts sending me bad ideas from its part of my brain, bad ideas masquerading as good ones. No. As *great* ones. And it's taken me a few laps around in Recovery Land to be able to pull the Scooby-Doo villain's mask off of the bad idea.

The lizard is always coming up with new disguises and tricks, so I remain vigilant.

Maybe it was this whole story, a kid being swept up in events outside of his control, that had me on a bit of an edge. Let's just say it resonated with my own personal history.

As I poured my coffee, I heard my phone ding. Careful not to spill my full coffee mug all over my hand, I fast-walked to the couch and my phone.

No text, but an email.

Sitting in my inbox was a file from Edward Stratton. He had finally gotten me the list of all the threatening emails and phone calls the Beverlys had received in the last year. There were over a thousand entries. I shouldn't have been surprised, but the sheer volume and vitriol knocked the wind out of me.

It seemed the people behind these threats didn't like the Beverlys for a multitude of reasons. Because they were billionaires. Because he was a venture capitalist. Because she was in charge of a family foundation that was "basically a tax haven."

I didn't think any of the critiques were necessarily wrong, just perhaps a little more colorful and violent than I would have made them. The Beverlys wealth was hard to imagine. And, to be frank, how much of a lifestyle difference was there between someone who had $100 million dollars and someone who had $4 billion? I could imagine losing my shit if someone tried to justify the difference as real.

Then again, we also have a habit of rewarding the wealthy with the pixie dust of legitimacy and authority, as if they made all the right choices to get where they got and we should look up to them for it.

As I scrolled through the list, I remembered another thing Gordon Bixby told me: We weren't there to judge the clients. We weren't even there to fix the clients — I had learned that one the hard way. We were there to do a job. Nothing more.

But me, not judging? A waste of a talent.

An idea ran through my mind. I could send the whole list to Matty. After all, he wanted to be a private detective, and I had warned him that it wasn't all glamour and fun. Maybe going through the list looking for suspects would show him what this job was really like.

I sighed and closed the file with a grunt.

What the hell was wrong with me? I'm the one who had

asked him to be my partner and now I wanted to give him the shit work. Had I made a mistake? The thing was, I was having a hard time taking him seriously.

I was doing to him what so many assholes had done to —

Ding. Another email. Nora had compiled the list of properties owned by Derrick Sayles. She's the best and I texted her a quick, *Thanks, you're the best.*

I then messaged Matty, filling him in on Ricky and then asked, *You want the list or the threat list?*

*Threat list?* he replied.

I sent back: *The list of all the emails and phone calls the Beverlys got in the last year.*

Another reply: *Property list. You can handle the crazies.* He ended it with a thumbs-up emoji.

All right then. I settled back into the couch and started sorting through them.

It was almost six o'clock when Dad came home. Something great must've happened because he floated in with the biggest grin. And a box of donuts. As he passed by me on the couch, I could hear his humming. "I have news," he announced as he dropped the box on my kitchenette's counter. He grabbed two bottles of water from the fridge and tossed me one.

I caught it with two hands.

Dad cracked his open and toasted me.

"What's the news?"

He licked his lips and opened the donut box. Snatching a chocolate frosted with sprinkles, he said, "We have a meeting." He took a bite and closed his eyes, enjoying every minute of it.

"A meeting? With who?"

He swallowed. "This is great. Oh my God. They don't have any good donuts in Vegas. Not like L.A."

"*Dad*."

"A couple of producers. They want to meet with you. They want to pitch you a project."

I groaned. "I don't have time for this kind of thing."

He wagged a finger at me, taking another bite of the donut. "No, no." He shook his head, chewing. "You said you would meet with people. You agreed."

I rolled my eyes. "OK, fine, *yes*, I agreed. If it's interesting —"

"Which it is."

"I'm in the middle of a case," I explained. "Right? In the middle. There's a kid out there, and I'm supposed to be finding him."

Stuffing the rest of the donut in his mouth, he mumbled something.

I shook my head at this fool. "What are you trying to say?"

He swallowed. "I said, if he's out there, why aren't you looking for him?"

I cracked open my bottle of water. "I should be driving

around L.A. looking for him? Shouting his name out the window? 'Patrick! Patrrriiiiiick!'" I took a drink. "That's not how it works."

His shoulders went to his ears. "How would I know how it works? I'm just saying, you say you got to find this kid and I see you here. So, in *my* mind" — he leaned against the counter — "you got time for a meeting."

"I'm narrowing things down."

He nodded. "Well, in between narrowing things, you can take a meeting. They want to meet this week. I told them Thursday."

The day before the exchange.

"Dad."

"It's *lunch*. You eat lunch while you're working a case, right?"

I rubbed my head. I could feel my case slipping away. "Yes," I acknowledged.

He spread his arms. "There you go. You take your lunch break Thursday afternoon, El Carmen on Third Street."

I closed my eyes. "Fine."

"It's going to be great," Dad said, stuffing another donut in his mouth. "But the big question is: What are we going to do for dinner?"

And with that, I forgot to even ask who I was meeting with and why. Paul Cooper always knew how to razzle dazzle me.

# 15

—

"YOU SEEM PREOCCUPIED," said Violet Ito as she sat across from me, holding her mug of coffee in the air.

It was Wednesday afternoon and it had already been a long, and probably wasted, day. And yeah, I *was* preoccupied. I smiled, shook my head, and picked at my scone. "No, no. Fully present."

Her head tilted. She didn't believe me.

I had been so excited to finally hang out with her not over a dead body and I was doing it all wrong.

We were in a cozy spot upstairs at a coffeeshop on Larchmont Avenue. Haim's cover of Fleetwood Mac's "Hold Me" bopped out of a hidden speaker. I had been late — and not even L.A. late, but *late* late — and found her waiting for me. I gave an apology without much explanation. She accepted it and a few minutes later we had our coffees and snacks. After we sat down, things got first-date-awkward. I asked her about her day and she told me how she and her partner broke up a ring of CraigsList thieves. I nodded along because it was the most amazing story ever.

When she finished, she asked about my day and I started thinking about what I could tell her.

I had spent the morning and a better part of the afternoon driving around the city interviewing other possible suspects, narrowed down from Stratton's threat list. None of which I could tell her.

Ito put the mug to her lips and looked over the rim. She took a sip and then said, "Are you working on a case?" She had come straight from work and wore her version of appropriate clothes for an LAPD Robbery-Homicide detective. She wore a designer T-shirt under her suit coat with her badge hanging off of her belt and black leather boots with a bit of a heel.

I shoved a piece of scone into my mouth and mumbled, "Kinda."

Her head tilted the other way, trying to make sense of what I had said.

I washed down the scone with some coffee. "Yeah, a case. Nothing exciting," I lied.

Suspect number one was John Pietersen. Actually, he was

third on my list, but the first who agreed to meet with me. We met up at a McDonald's on Whittier Boulevard in Boyle Heights. Glamor ends at downtown. The neighborhood was working class and mostly Mexican-American. It's the part of L.A. they don't really put in travel guides.

John was a white guy in his sixties with a bushy white beard. His eyes were dark brown, almost black, and the way he looked at me could peel the skin right off your bones. And his fists were like hammers as he banged on the table explaining how Robert Beverly was responsible for shutting down the factory John had worked at for decades. He was out of a job and given his age and skill set, his future didn't look great. And over the past year, he has sent several emails to the Beverlys making it clear how much he blamed them for his situation.

Ito put down her coffee and laced her fingers together. "OK, let's get real."

I shifted in my seat, worried.

"What's it been like the past few weeks? After all that good press from the last case, you must've gotten some crazy awesome opportunities."

"Nothing *so* crazy," I said, a little relieved.

I had gotten John to talk to me because I had lied to him. I had told him that Cooper and Associates was representing someone else who had sent threats to the Beverlys and had been harassed by the police. John was excited to tell me his story.

"There have been meetings," I finally said to her.

"Meetings?" Violet replied. "Very mysterious."

I shrugged. "Do we have to talk about work?"

She shook her head and smiled. It was beautiful.

John Pietersen told me how his father had been a Sixties Radical. "Not a hippie, but a *radical*." And that he thought the whole system was shit and the little guy was always getting screwed. I thought, yeah, maybe. And maybe $50 million dollars would go a long way. Then he told me how he had been in Palm Desert for the past two weeks to take care of his granddaughter while his daughter tried to figure out medical care after hurting her arm at work.

I thanked him, telling him I had everything I needed and to take care of himself. He was desperate, and it broke my heart. There wasn't much I could really do for him. Even if I could get Mom involved, which I could, what he really wanted couldn't happen. He wasn't going to get his old life back. That was the fucking tragedy of it all.

"Have you seen any good movies lately?" I asked Violet before realizing what a cheesy question that was.

Thankfully, she laughed. "No. I haven't. Have you?"

"Does *Commando* count?"

Her face squished. "It does not."

I gasped, offended.

Suspect number two was in Glendale. This one had been at

the top of my list and he worked at a Home Depot there. He had become obsessed with the Beverlys a few years ago. He imagined himself as a financial guru after having amassed a not insignificant following on social media and had hopes of working for Robert's company. When he was rejected, he kept up the harassment. Surprisingly, the Beverly group continued to not hire him and reported him to the police and got a restraining order.

I spotted my guy in the lumber section. He was smaller than either of the guys in the video with Patrick. And skinny. And then there was the broken leg in a walking cast. Not my guy.

"Then what *is* a good movie?" I asked Violet.

She shrugged. "Are we talking action movies?"

"If you don't like *Commando*, you must not like action movies."

Violet laughed. "OK, Jimmy, those sounds like fighting words. Don't like action movies? Whatever."

Grabbing my coffee, I said, "What does make a good action movie then?"

"It's obvious, right?" she said, leaning back. "Anything with Jackie Chan."

"Anything?" I challenged.

She nodded.

I cleared my throat. "*Cannonball Run.*"

Violet paused. "The exception that proves the rule."

I laughed at that.

Suspect number three had been fourth on my list as I still hadn't tracked down number two. And she was the first woman on my list. As I crossed the Los Angeles River on Glendale Boulevard, I started thinking there had to be a better way to go about this; maybe another way to track down the kidnappers than going down a list. They wanted their payment in diamonds. And there are very few places you can walk into, exchange $50 million worth of diamonds, and come out with cash. These diamond were going to be hot.

They would need a fence. Someone who could turn those diamonds into cash.

A fence that would be able to get them the most value for the diamonds. For ten to fifteen percent. In L.A., everyone takes a percentage.

And I did know a guy.

Someone that I had been sort of avoiding.

OK. Totally avoiding.

When I was inbetween careers — meaning when I was really in the depths of my addictions — I traveled in some, shall we say, shadier circles. Listen, don't judge me. I was doing enough of some substances that I couldn't keep going to a doctor for a refill without making them suspicious. I had to turn to other sources. And I'm a naturally curious guy, so I met *lots* of people.

Now, to be clear, and because my lawyer sister would insist on it, I did nothing *that* illegal. I met some people who did. Some scary people. People I would not want to piss off, so I was "friendly" with them.

One guy in particular, let's call him a "former business associate," might know someone who could fence that amount of hot rocks. Of course, he's the one I had been trying to avoid.

"What's going on?" asked Violet.

"What do you mean?" I said, finishing off my coffee.

She leaned back and frowned. "You keep like, I don't know, disappearing. You're here, but you're not."

I grunted. "This is a pretty terrible first date, huh?"

"Not what I was hoping," she said. "But I've had worse."

I nodded. "Same. All I'll say is that mine ended with the *almost* torching the Hollywood Sign."

"You stopped it?"

I frowned. "Yeah. Let's go with that." I grinned.

Violet nodded, laughed. She waved her empty mug and said she was getting a refill and wondered if I wanted another. I shook my head no.

Number three had been a part of a political action group that had a problem with the Beverly Foundation. She didn't feel they were doing enough for housing and education. Turns out, she was in recovery in a halfway house in Koreatown. She had served some time for assault. She admitted to a drinking problem, which had also contributed to her rash decisions to send threats to the Beverlys. She said she had been there for the past month. To be sure, I checked the logs. Sure enough, she had an alibi.

After that, desperate, I sat in my car and called the guy. It went straight to voicemail.

"This is Danny," a deep voice on the outgoing message announced. And then there was a beep. Danny was always to the point. He did not bullshit around.

"Danny! It's Jimmy. Haven't talked to you in a while."

While he had kept his hand in the scene, Danny had been lying low for the past few years, trying to avoid some heat. Someone may or may not have spilled some information about operations peripheral to his work in order to get time served, thereby sending a bunch of other people to jail and putting a bunch of others at risk.

Spoilers: It was me. I spilled a name or two. I wasn't built for prison.

"I was wondering if you knew anyone who could fence diamonds. Like a lot of diamonds." I paused, realizing what my message sounded like. "Asking for a friend! A screenwriter! He wants some, you know, authenticity for... for a screenplay. This is totally a fiction, made-up ask." Nailed it. I left my phone number and hung up. I saw the time and realized I was going to be really late meeting Ito.

While I waited for her to come back with her refill, my

phone dinged. I pulled it out of my suit coat pocket. It was a text from Patrick's friend, Blake. He was finally getting back to me about Derrick.

*Nope. Don't remember either of those dudes at the party.*

Shit. It didn't mean that Derrick wasn't involved. But —

"Everything, OK?"

I looked up. Violet was back and sitting down.

"Fine, fine," I said, lying again.

"You don't look fine," she said, sitting. "What's going on?"

I looked at her. I could tell her I was working on a case. It wouldn't be weird. It was my job after all. And *then* I could tell her that I couldn't talk about it. And the truth was I wanted to tell her. Every single detail. Patrick's life was in danger and it was Wednesday and I was fucked. If I told her, then maybe she could save him. But I had agreed to keep my dumb mouth shut.

"It's Mom," I said. I couldn't believe how much I was lying. "She wants me to run an errand for her."

Ito nodded. She didn't believe me.

I jumped as my phone rang in my hand. Danny was calling me back. Ito eyed the phone and then looked at me. "If it's important, you should take it."

The phone rang again.

"It's important," I admitted. "It's work."

She nodded. "Let's do this another time then." Ito stood

up, coffee in hand. I reached out to stop her, but the phone kept ringing. She shook her head. "You better answer it."

And I did as I watched her head down the stairs.

"Why do you still have this number?" a deep voice spoke slowly, making sure I could really hear what he was saying, which translated to, *You should've lost this number years ago.*

Ito asked for and got a paper cup from the barista.

I looked away. "You never know when I'll need to talk to you," I said, trying to sound upbeat. I watched as she poured the rest into the cup, pushed on a plastic lid and headed out without looking back.

Danny grunted. I took that as permission to keep talking.

"I just need this favor." I looked at my empty mug and wished I hadn't answered the phone.

"That's pretty nervy of you," he said.

"You know me."

I could hear him shift, his face rubbing against the phone as he said with a sigh, "This isn't about a screenplay, is it?"

"No. It's a case."

Another dose of silence. "Are the cops involved?"

"Lucky for you, no. No cops are involved." I wondered if I had fucked things up with Ito. "I'm just looking for some names. I need to know someone who could fence a big job."

Danny cleared his throat. "And if I give you a name and you find these people, what's going to happen to them?" He was concerned about sticking his neck out too much.

"Listen," I said. "I'm just looking for someone. The cops are not involved. It's just me." I did not tell him about Matty. I was having enough trouble convincing him to trust me. "My client wants to keep things quiet."

Danny thought about it. "Information, as you know, costs, Jimmy."

"Of course." Good thing the Beverlys were paying well.

"Was it you?" asked Danny.

I stopped moving. I looked around. A couple of other tables were occupied. Two women chatted over lattes. A man in the corner was working on a laptop with headphones on. He was totally working on a screenplay. "Was what me?" I managed.

"Did you rat out Eric?" asked Danny.

Oh, shit. He was still trying to figure out who had narc'd and cost him money.

"You there?" said Danny.

"I'm here." What was I going to tell him? Shit, shit, shit.

"Did you rat — "

"Yes." Fuck it. "I did rat on Eric. I cut a deal to stay out of jail. Simple as that."

One of the two women glanced at me. I waved at her and turned away. I didn't need prying eyes as I confessed an old sin.

Danny didn't say anything. I worried that he had hung up and was already tracking my phone and sending some muscle to pick me up. Was I sweating? Yeah, I was sweating.

Finally: "Eric was an asshole," said Danny.

I gulped in air. I hadn't realized I had stopped breathing.

"That took some balls, telling me the truth, but Eric deserved what he had coming. He was always bad at business." He laughed. "OK. I'll ask some questions, Jimmy. I'll get back to you."

"Does this mean we're even?" I ventured.

"You and me?" He paused. "Hell no."

# 16

———

THURSDAY AFTERNOON, I was sitting in a Mexican restaurant across from two producers talking about a job. It was a little over a day until the exchange for Patrick's life, and me and Matty hadn't come up with anything substantial.

Sorry. I'm overselling it.

We had come up with nothing.

I had gone further down my list, interviewing two more people that morning who had nothing to do with Patrick, while Matty focused on Derrick Sayles. Ultimately, we weren't any closer, and my promise to the Beverlys, that I would find their son, was slipping away. I hated that I didn't spill the beans on the whole thing yesterday with Ito. Maybe if the police had been involved from the very beginning there would've been real movement on the case.

And I had been up all night thinking about what a disaster the coffee date had been.

But at least the nachos were good.

El Carmen was on Third Street, about a fifteen-minute walk from CBS Television City and the Farmer's Market. The space was longer than it was wide with a curved, tiled ceiling. On one side was a long bar; on the other were square tables with bench seating along the wall. Multicolored Christmas lights were looped throughout. Two large, metal ceiling fans churned the air, and hung around the walls were *luchadores* in various victorious poses.

I snatched another chip from the plate between us as the producers finished up their pitch. The producer across from me on my right was a woman named Gail. She was tall, somewhere in her thirties, wore glasses and a bright yellow sweater, even though the weather was in the lower eighties. Michael on my left was Asian American, both a little older and a little shorter than Gail, and he wore a suit with a T-shirt. They had tag-teamed the pitch. Michael was super excited, and Gail would always ground the pitch with some cool idea. But in the end...

"A game show?" I said in between bites. Not exactly where I thought this meeting was going. *This* was what Dad wanted to surprise me with? *This* was the interesting idea? I had hoped it would be a single-camera comedy or something.

From his seat next to me, Dad came back with, "It's

a *classic* game show. I loved it as a kid." He looked at me. "You'd be perfect as a panelist." He turned to the producers. "I'm so jazzed you're bringing it back."

A celebrity panelist. Hm. I thought about Joan Rivers and Jim J. Bullock stuck inside their respective boxes on the *Hollywood Squares*.

Before the meeting had started, my father hadn't prepared me. In fact, he had done just the opposite.

Standing outside the place, he had said, "You have to be yourself."

"Listen with an open mind," he had *also* said.

And he had finished with, "This is network."

OK, then. Network meant a big payday. I got why he was so excited.

I shoved another chip into my mouth. "I don't know if I'm a game show sort of guy," I said, much to Dad's consternation. He grabbed his beer and drank, hoping to cover his disappointment with me.

Michael nodded, saying, "Sure, sure. But, like your dad said, it's a revival. So it's not just a game show; it's packed with love and nostalgia."

"It's a show families can watch together," added Gail.

"It's generational," Michael threw in. "It's going to be huge."

Our tacos arrived before I could point out that was a lot of nonsense.

Gail unrolled her flatware. "It's going to be fun. That's the focus. Fun. Who doesn't want to watch fun?"

Michael laughed. "And we're going to be giving away so much money," he said, then dug into his carne asada taco.

Gail bit more daintily into hers. "So much," she mumbled, putting a hand to her mouth before crumbs could fall out.

"But you'll save enough to pay the celebrities, right?" Dad spoke with a wink.

They all laughed, but he was also dead serious.

This is how negotiations begin in Hollywood, with smiles and laughter. It's only later that the knives come out.

Gail looked at me and said, "It's going to be a great gig for you. We'll shoot, like, four episodes a day, twice a week. Super easy. Just be you."

I glanced at Dad. "That sounds familiar."

The producers looked at him, sensing something was wrong.

"Is there a problem?" asked Gail.

"We hope there isn't a problem," Michael echoed.

Dad put down his half-eaten shrimp taco. "There's no problem," he assured them. "He's working a case, so he's a little distracted."

I pushed my plate back, annoyed. I didn't want to talk about the case in public.

Both of the producers, however, lit up. An "ooooh" escaped from Michael, and Gail nodded with excitement.

"Tell us everything," said Michael, taking another bite.

Gail looked at him. "This will be great fodder for the host."

"Right?" he agreed.

My phone buzzed.

Dad asked, "Who are you thinking of?"

"We're thinking of getting," Gail started, then held up a finger as she took a gulp of Sprite.

"It's a dream host," said Michael.

My phone buzzed again, and I dug it out of my suit coat.

Gail swallowed and said, "Kevin Hart."

Phone in hand, I looked at the producers. Kevin Hart? These guys weren't going to get Kevin Hart to do a gameshow. Were they?

My phone buzzed again.

"We've approached his people," explained Michael. "I went to school with a guy on his team, so it's a legit approach."

"Kevin would eat this stuff up," Gail said, bolstering Michael's enthusiasm.

I looked at my phone. Matty was calling. Now, of all times. Great.

"I gotta take this," I said, waving the phone, but I didn't move. What if I was going to miss something? I shook my head. I need to focus. I was on a *case*. "And no, I can't talk about it. The case. It's, you know, unresolved."

Paul frowned. "Come on, Jimmy, you can at least tell

them it's a kidnapping."

Gail gasped.

"*Dad.*" I glared at my father.

Michael's eyes went wide. "Is it someone we know?"

I gave a big shrug rather than answering. I stood and stepped through the restaurants's red-lacquered door, answering as soon as I hit the sidewalk.

"Matty, what's up?"

"Jimmy, it's a dead end."

"What? What's a dead — "

"Sayles. Sayles didn't have anything to do with it."

I dodged a group of friends heading somewhere for lunch, so that I stood closer to the curb.

"Are you sure?" I asked, squirming. I hated that I had left my sunglasses at the table.

"Of course I'm *sure.*"

I shook my head. "How do you know?"

"I know because," he said bluntly, "I checked his social calendar. And I've checked most of his properties."

I put up a finger. "There's still Ricky."

Dad stepped out of the restaurant and waved his arms at me. I shooed him away, trying to get him to go back inside.

He put his hands on his hips, bothered. He hooked a thumb back at the restaurant. "They're waiting," he mouthed.

I covered my phone. "I'm in the middle of something," I seethed.

"I know," he said. "I'm in the middle of it too."

I pointed at my phone. "This. *This* is what I'm in the middle of."

Dad shook his head like I was the one being unreasonable.

"Are you listening?" asked Matty.

Had Matty been talking?

"I am, I am," I said as I turned my back on my dad. "Can you just repeat it?"

Matty groaned. "Ricky Johnson was eighty miles away the night Patrick was kidnapped. He was up at Lake Arrowhead, camping." Before I could question it, Matty added, "*Yes*, I confirmed it."

Shitballs.

"So, what do we do now?" he asked.

I paced a bit. "We keep going down my list."

"Your list of crazy people?" He sounded frustrated.

"They are not all crazy. But, yeah. It's what we've got."

"Fuck." He hung up, and I went back inside, where Dad was entertaining the producers. They were all smiles and giggles.

Gail was the first to see me. "Any developments in the case?"

I kept mum and sat back down. I stared at my tacos, not hungry anymore.

"This is great," said Michael. "When you're on the panel with us, you'll still be a working private investigator — your dad told us how important that was to you — ”

Dad waved.

“So it can be this thing,” Michael continued, “between you and Kevin.”

Gail jumped in. “Kevin would go crazy for it. I can see a whole bit being developed around that. Like, he asks questions, and you can't answer. He gets all upset and crazy the way that he does because he's so frustrated with you.”

My eyes unfocused from the tacos and refocused on Gail's pastel-framed glasses. “A bit?” I said.

“*To*-tally a bit.”

She had my attention. I *loved* doing bits and running gags. When I used to do talk shows, my banter *killed*. And they want me to do that with a big star?

“So, what do you think, Jimmy? Something you'd be interested in doing?”

Dad looked at me, eyebrows hopeful.

I know I should've been thinking about the case and Patrick and how terrified he probably was, wherever he was trapped, but I kept circling back to Kevin Hart looking at me, grinning as he just delivered a well-timed rant I could deliver a comeback to. Then he would pull a face, the audience would whoop, and then he'd “move on,” which would be hilarious because he's a fucking genius.

“Sure,” I said, playing it cool. “I'm interested. Could be fun.”

# 17

——

"SO YOU *BOTH* failed," said Robert Beverly, the ice in his rocks glass shaking. "Spectacularly."

It was Friday afternoon, maybe only a couple of hours away from the exchange. Matty and I sat on the leather couch in the Beverlys' living room. Away from the ocean view, the room had clean, white marble floors with Turkish rugs. More expensive paintings — was that a Monet? — hung on the walls.

Or was this a parlor? Maybe it was a parlor. Do people still have parlors? I was having a hard time focusing.

Matty put up a finger. "I didn't fail. I just haven't succeeded yet."

While I admired his bravado, Robert did not.

He aimed a finger at Matty and said, "Go fuck yourself, Mr. Goodman." Another rattle of the glass was followed by another gulp of whiskey.

To our right, Eva Beverly sat in an accent chair. "You've run out of time," she snapped.

We had. We had run around the city and turned up nothing. There were lots of people who might have wanted to take Patrick, but we hadn't gotten anywhere close to finding him. I felt terrible, and the lecture from Scrooge McDuck wasn't helping.

"That's not my fault," replied Matty.

I shook my head. He wasn't going to get anywhere being defensive. Even if he was right. I gave it a go. "Yeah, we ran out time, and yeah, we didn't find him. That was always going to be a possibility. Especially with one hand tied behind our backs." I sighed, realizing this was *(a)* probably not the most comforting thing to say and *(b)* it was coming off as an excuse. "It's still not too late to call the police."

Eva looked at her husband, who finished off his drink and headed back to the drink cart.

"No," he uttered. I knew he was under stress, but I wondered if the drinking was going to help. "We're not calling them," he said. "We'll just see this through to the end. We have the money. We have everything they asked for."

I crossed my arms. Robert Beverly was a stubborn asshole,

but he was writing the checks so he ultimately called the shots. The plan was for Matty and me to go and do the exchange. Robert was going to get his money's worth out of us.

I just hoped Patrick would survive it.

Eva looked unhappy and angry. Unhappy with us, angry with her husband. It had been a couple of days since I had seen either one of them, and they both looked rather worse for wear. I could see the strain this situation was putting on their relationship. They were barely looking at each other.

Having refilled, Robert announced to the room, "Once Patrick is back and safe, we'll deal with whoever did this."

Matty shifted on the couch, and I looked at Eva. "Deal?" I asked.

"You mean, like," Matty whispered, "*deal*?"

Robert's eyes narrowed. "It's not something that you two need to worry about."

Matty gave me a side-eye. I wondered if this conversation was going to take an awkward and illegal turn.

"Whatever happens," Eva said to us, "whatever they want, just give it to them. I want my son back."

"Of course, Mrs. Beverly," I answered her with a grim smile.

Robert looked up from his glass as Edward Stratton stepped into the room. He came over and whispered into Robert's ear. Robert nodded and left the room with his head of security, who gave me a strange look on the way out.

"What's going on?" I asked Eva.

She turned her eyes back to me. "It's here."

I took a breath and exhaled slowly. The "it" in question was the $50 million in diamonds.

---

THE NEXT FEW hours were rough for the Beverlys, as they waited for the phone to ring. Everything was quiet. Conversations were conducted in hushed whispers, if there was any talking at all.

Matty bided his time by the pool, staring out at the ocean. He chewed on his thumbnail as his left leg bobbed up and down. I asked him if he was OK, if he was nervous about tonight. He shook his head quickly, leg still bouncing. Something felt off, but Matty wasn't interested in talking.

Robert and Edward had secluded themselves in Robert's office and clearly weren't interested in talking to me. Go figure. You don't find one kid before their kidnapping deadline, and suddenly you're persona non grata.

I had no idea where Eva was.

To keep busy — and keep the lizard at bay — I started wandering the house.

The staff didn't say anything as I moved from room to room to room. Maybe they didn't give a shit, given the circumstances. There were a lot of rooms in this place. Life here was not small. And while I liked my cozy bungalow, I could get used to the idea of having a dining room separate from the space where I watched TV.

I gazed into a whole room dedicated to storing wine. As a recovering alcoholic I wasn't tempted, but confused. When I was drinking, storage wasn't necessary. Who had time to store when there was drinking to be done?

After checking out all the amenities on the first floor, I headed up the curved stairway, gazing at the large, crystal chandelier hanging from the glass ceiling. I felt like a princess. Upstairs, it felt more secluded than the open spaces below. There were more doors — big, tall, regal doors off a large main hallway. I turned left and stopped at the first one. It was closed.

And, as someone who is hired to snoop, that's practically an invitation.

I put my hand on the brass handle and peeked down the hall, just to make sure no one was about to pop out and wag their finger at me. Empty. I pulled the handle and stepped inside.

There was no mistaking that this was Patrick's room. My jaw dropped because it felt larger than my bungalow. A king-size bed was centered between two large windows whose curtains were partially drawn, adding a bit of gloom to the room as the evening approached. On the walls, nicely framed, were vintage posters of rock shows. Some of them were pretty expensive. In a corner, a Fender guitar had gathered dust.

Also mounted on the wall were three katanas with a pair of sai hanging next to them.

Rich kids and their hobbies.

I heard a shuddering breath come from the bathroom. Looking in, I found Eva, sitting on the toilet, clutching a teddy bear. Hearing me, she looked up, her eyes wet.

My hands went up, and I started making apology noises.

She stood, and I realized she wasn't using the toilet for anything more than a seat.

"Sorry, sorry," I still said. "I can..." I pointed to the way out of this uncomfortable moment.

"No, no," she said, wiping her eyes. She glanced at the bear in her hands. "It's Patrick's," she said, explaining her embarrassment. "When he was..." She walked past me into the bedroom and put the bear back onto a bookshelf. She turned to me and said, "You don't have any kids, do you?"

I shook my head no.

She nodded quickly, blew out air through pursed lips. "This is one of the many nightmares I've had ever since he was born. There's a lot of joy in being a parent. A lot. But it all comes with, 'What if it goes wrong?' And here we are." Eva's legs gave out, and she sat on the edge of the bed. "Patrick was always braver than I was. I never had to push him to try new things. He would always run ahead of me. Always be the first to the top of the slide. First jumping into the pool." She smiled at the memory. "I would try and help him with something and he would tell me, 'I *know*, Mommy.'" She looked up at me. "Later, as he got older, he needed me even less and less. It's hard not to think of him as still a little kid." She paused. "I hope he's being brave right now."

Before I could tell her anything, a phone rang in the distance. She caught her breath and left the room.

I followed her down the stairs as the phone kept ringing. Eva turned and headed toward Robert's office. I was halfway there when one of the bathroom doors opened and Matty stepped out. He shifted his eyes away from me toward Robert's office, and his hand went to his pants pocket. "Is that them? Are they calling?" He swallowed.

"Yeah."

He nodded to me, I nodded to him, and we both headed to the office.

We ended up just inside the doorway. Robert was standing behind his desk, holding the receiver to his ear. Edward was next to him, and Eva stood braced between the two men, hands clasped together nervously.

"I want proof that he's still alive," demanded Robert.

Eva flinched at that. She wanted to know if her son was OK, and here we were, asking if he was *alive*.

Robert tried again, louder. "I want — "

He was cut off, then said, "Yes, yes. We have it. Now — "

Cut off again, he fumed. He nodded and snatched a pen out of its holder and started writing. Edward looked up at me and Matty. There was a lot of looking going on, and I felt like I was being left out of the loop. I didn't like that.

"Yes," said Robert, his voice tighter. He paused. "Forty-five minutes?" He looked at Edward, pointing to whatever he wrote. Edward shook his head. "They can't make it in — "

From the look on Robert Beverly's face, they had hung up. He put the phone down and leaned against the desk on his fists.

Edward spoke to Matty and me. "The exchange is going to be at a Park and Ride in Encino. You have forty-five minutes to get there."

Encino from the Pacific Palisades? Shit. Evening was here, and rush hour was still going strong.

Edward lifted a black briefcase from beside the desk and walked it over to us. "It's all in here." And he held it out. Matty's eyes flickered from Edward to Robert, from Eva to me. He didn't want to touch it.

Like it was radioactive material, I took the briefcase.

I held it in one hand and clicked it open with the other, one latch at a time. Inside, under black velvet, were diamonds, all still mounted into jewelry. I'm pretty sure I had seen one of them around Halle Berry's neck at the Oscars. They say money can't buy you love, but Patrick Beverly could probably have made a decent rebuttal. His parents must have called in a lot of favors around town to get this haul.

Edward snapped the case closed.

"I said you had forty-five minutes. Why are you still here?" He handed me the piece of the paper where Robert had scribbled the address. The hint was obvious.

I turned and left, Matty in tow.

Outside, we walked toward my car, which looked ludicrously out of place here.

"We should put a tracker in there," offered Matty.

I raised an eyebrow.

"Yeah, a tracker," he doubled down. "So we can follow them."

"We're not following them." I unlocked my car and put the case in the backseat. "We're bringing Patrick right back here."

"For later," he insisted.

I shook my head. "There isn't a later. We were paid to find Patrick. We know where he is." I wiggled the note in the air. "Case is done."

"If we *track* them — "

I slammed the back door closed. "Do you have a tracker?"

As Matty scrambled for an idea, I wondered if this was more than nerves. Then, he had an idea. "My phone." He pointed at the back seat. "We'll put my phone in there. We'll track these motherfuckers."

Motherfuckers?

I paused. "This isn't fun and games, Matty. We're so close to having a happy ending. Let's not screw it up, OK?"

He tapped his fingers on the roof of my car, then finally: "Fine. Whatever." He opened the passenger-side door and got in.

I shook my head and slid into my seat. The car started, and Ten Years After's "I'd Love To Change the World" played as we headed away from the Beverlys, north on the 405 and, hopefully, on to Patrick.

# 18

—

"IT'S A TACTICAL vest," Matty was explaining. His eyes stared out into the darkness of the parking lot. They were wide and unblinking, like he was trying to take in everything all at once. I thought he was about to jump out of his skin. "The vest has everything that I need."

Except a shirt, apparently.

Once Matty was in the passenger seat and we had peeled out of the Beverlys' driveway, he had changed into the vest, wearing nothing underneath. Matty still worked out and had a bunch of tattoos up and down his arms and onto his chest. I envied him. One, the tats did make him look badass, and two, he had the discipline to get his ass to the gym.

We had arrived with a couple of minutes to spare. Just off

the 101, the Park and Ride was a lot you could leave your car while you rode into work with a coworker. A bold plan to get cars off the roads.

Spoilers: There were more cars than ever in the city.

Which meant the lot was pretty much empty. We were parked in a corner with pools of light dotting the way to the entrance. The only sound was "Mouhamabou Bamba" by Orchestra Baobab coming quietly out of my car's speakers.

Annoyed, I asked him, "What do you need in that vest that you can't put in a pocket?"

"It has everything, Jimmy, that I need, OK?" He looked at me. His eyes were dilated. Shit. I no longer thought that he was vigilant.

"Are you high right now?" It would explain that moment outside the bathroom at the Beverlys'. And the whole afternoon.

He shook his head, still looking out into the parking lot. "I took some Adderall, that's it."

Adderall. Shit, shit.

I turned to look fully at him. "What the fuck, Matty?" I did not need this wild card. Not when we were this close. I had rehearsed everything in my mind. I had gone over how it should go. Just like Gordon had taught me. And now this.

He gawked back at me. "Why don't you focus on the job and let me handle my shit?"

"Your *shit*?" I couldn't believe this. "At least I'm not high right now."

"I'm not *high*. I am prepared. I'm ready for whatever they got coming for me."

"Do you even hear yourself?" I started to wonder if this was connected to what had happened to him with Sayles's bodyguard outside his apartment.

He looked back out through the windshield. "Of course I hear myself. I hear everything right now." He looked at me with a raised eyebrow. "I hear you being a little bitch about me taking Adderall."

Frustrated, I snapped, "I'm not a little bitch. I just don't think you should be high right now." He was about to correct me, so I corrected myself. "Sorry. *Abusing* ADHD medication. Better?"

He grunted and brought his attention back to the parking lot.

I rubbed the side of my head and leaned against the doorframe. This whole conversation was making me nervous. I didn't like the fact we had $50 million sitting in the back seat of a car worth $3,000 and my partner was a jacked-up — I looked at Matty — weirdo. No ifs, ands or buts about it. He was a jacked-up weirdo.

It was fine. It was *fine*. Things were going to turn out OK. I would take care of everything, I'd give them the case, and they would give me Patrick. The end.

"Car." Matty pointed past me. I swatted away his hand

and looked. Sure enough, a car was coming. Matty started breathing in through his nose and blowing out through his mouth.

"What are you *doing*?"

"I'm filling my body with oxygen." In through the nose, out through the mouth.

I shook my head. "You don't need to do that. You're going to hyperventilate."

That car passed by and kept going.

"See? Wasn't our car."

Matty darted around and kept an eye on it. "It's going to turn around." There was an edge to his voice. "He wants to make sure we're alone." He looked at me. "That we didn't bring in cops."

"Sure, Matty, sure." As if I didn't know what I was talking about.

The car turned around. *Dammit.* Matty was right. He grinned at me.

The car parked about twenty feet away, facing us. The front side window was tinted, so I couldn't see inside. The headlights flashed. I took a breath, turned off the music, and turned to Matty.

Before I could tell him to chill the fuck out and that I would handle everything, he had stepped out of the car and slammed the door behind him. I reached back, grabbed the briefcase, and clumsily brought it forward. Getting out of the car, I walked to the front. Matty was posed, legs wide, hands gripping the tactical vest. He focused deeply on the car, like he was daring it to fuck with him.

The driver's-side door opened. Briefly the interior light went on, and I strained to see if Patrick was in the back or if I could see anyone else in there.

The driver wore black jeans and a black sweatshirt, and their face was hidden under a ski mask. I asked myself where they had gotten a ski mask in L.A. this time of the year. OK, the answer was probably Amazon. Then I thought I should really focus on the present situation.

"I'll take that," the driver said, pointing to the briefcase. Their voice was all gravely and super serious. They were clearly trying to disguise it, like Batman or something.

*Just be cool, Jimmy,* I told myself. *Just be cool.*

I had taken a half step forward when Matty put a hand up, stopping me. "Not until we see the package."

Jesus. The *package*? What sort of network television nightmare was I living in? Even the driver was confused, his head tipping as he looked at Matty.

Matty clarified. "I want to see that Patrick Beverly is alive and well."

The driver put up a cautionary finger. "You don't get to make demands here."

Matty took a step forward, balling his fists.

Putting a hand on his shoulder, I said, "Can we do this

without all this macho stuff?"

Matty pulled his shoulder away, not even bothering to look at me.

I tried again. "I got this." I stepped in front of Matty, the suave cop to his bad boy. I said to the driver, "How are you? Lovely night to end a kidnapping."

The driver looked around, wondering just what the fuck was I doing. Great question. I kept tumbling forward. "My aggressive partner is right. It would be great to see Patrick. We wouldn't want to turn over so many... Look, there's a lot of diamonds here." Keep it together, Jimmy. "It's all here. The amount you asked for. But I would — *we* would — be in a lot of trouble if we handed them over and you drove off without us having an alive Patrick to bring back to his parents. I don't have malpractice insurance to cover that sort of screwup."

I smiled. Smiles are always disarming in the tensest of situations. Try it sometime.

The driver thought about it. Then he leaned back and pounded the glass. The rear window rolled down, and sure enough, there was Patrick, tape over his mouth sitting inside the dark car.

"We good?" said the driver in his fake-ass voice.

"Sure." I took another step forward, then paused. "So, what's the plan? I hand this to you, you'll open the door? Or, you know, you open the door now then I hand you the case?"

The driver tensed up. I could feel Matty getting tense too. Ask clarifying questions and everyone gets nervous…

"Guys. This is a transaction. A business deal," I explained. Sure, this was a federal crime, but for the most part, yeah, a business deal.

I walked closer to the driver, extending the case. He was wearing black latex gloves. He reached out for the case and —

The driver was on the ground, Matty on top of him. He had tackled him for some unknown reason. There was a struggle, as both men tried to punch each other. I moved around them, trying not to yell, trying to figure out how I could stop this without drawing a police presence, and my back was to the kidnapper's car. I heard the car door open, a partner stepping out —

My head ringing, I was on the ground too and the world was a carousel. I felt like throwing up.

Something was snatched from my hand. What was pulled from my hand?

I heard shouting.

A car peeled away.

Someone was saying something over and over. I managed to get to my feet and turn.

Matty. It was Matty. He was on the ground in a pool of light. "*Fuck*!" he was shouting. He was holding his stomach.

I looked at my hands. They were empty. The briefcase. They took the briefcase. And they still had Patrick.

"Shit." I stumbled toward Matty as the concrete rose and dropped in front of me. "Matty… they took it, they took…"

As I got closer to Matty, I could see it. All the blood pouring out from underneath his stupid vest. I knelt beside him and unzipped it and there was more blood all over his chest. Fuck me, fuck me.

I put my hands on top of his, over the wound — *wounds*, there were multiple wounds. We held hands as he kept bleeding. The blood was warm, but it was cooling. Matty was mumbling and struggling.

I didn't hear a gunshot. He must've been stabbed. "Just keep still, Matty. It's going to be fine; it's going to be fine." I wondered how I was going to call 911 when I couldn't take my hands off his guts or he would bleed out. Maybe someone was going to come by. It was a parking lot. Surely someone needed to park. Maybe another meeting of kidnappers was going to take place. This was as good a place as any for a drop. The 101 was right there.

So I shouted. "Help! Help me! Someone! Help!" It was at the top of my lungs. I screamed and screamed as Matty moved less and less. I could hear clicking sounds as he tried to breathe.

He stopped moving. His eyes looked at me like they were saying, "Why didn't you warn me?"

Fuck you, Matty. Fuck you. I *told* you not to do this.

I stood up when I realized there wasn't anything left I could do for him. I shouted at him. I screamed at his body about how stupid he was. I shouted about how beautiful life was and if he had taken my advice at the party, maybe he could be doing commercials again and maybe he could have had a chance at a real comeback. After all the shouting was done, nothing changed. He was gone and I felt empty.

Exhausted, I fell to the ground, flat on my ass. I wiped my blood-covered hands on my suit before reaching into my coat pocket. I grabbed my phone. My fingers slipped and left prints all over it. I wiped my hands again, finally able to dial 911.

# 19

—

MATTY WAS DEAD.

Red and blue lights flickered in the night. Ten minutes after I called them, eleven minutes after Matty had stopped moving, cop cars had roared into the parking lot, followed by an ambulance. I sat on the trunk of my car, my back to it all. Behind me, the cops collected evidence under the bright lights they had set up. Matty was in the center of it all, covered with a white sheet.

My sticky hands shook as I held on to my phone. I had just called the Beverlys and explained how it all became a clusterfuck and that the police were now involved whether they liked it or not. Robert hung up on me without so much as a thank you for the heads-up. I didn't blame him, but it would've been nice.

A car pulled up outside the yellow tape, two familiar faces peering through the windshield. I had dreaded this more than calling the Beverlys. Detective Kemble, thick-bodied and with a high and tight haircut that was more salt than pepper, lumbered out of the car. I could see in his eyes that he wasn't thrilled to see me. His partner, though, looked disappointed.

Ito was in a leather jacket, T-shirt, jeans and combats boots; her badge hung down from her neck. The way she looked at me... I instantly regretted every lie I had told her on our coffee date and every moment she wagged her finger at me was going to be terrible, but the way she looked at me still made my heart skip a little. Even though it was all shit around me, I was glad she was the one assigned to the call.

"Every time you're around," rumbled Kemble as he got closer, "I get the worst heartburn."

I nodded. "Same. And I can only imagine what your ex-wives went through."

Kemble squeezed his lips together and huffed through his nose. Deciding not to punch me, he asked, "Who's your friend?"

"He isn't — wasn't a friend."

"Coworker?" asked Kemble.

I looked over at Ito, wondering why she hadn't said anything yet.

"Hey, idiot, I asked you — "

"Sure, Kemble. A coworker." I shook my head. "Matty shouldn't have been here. He was just an actor."

"Matty?" said Kemble.

"Matty Goodman, yeah."

"Oh, shit," Ito murmured. "My little sister loved him."

Kemble looked at her for a second and then asked me, "What happened?"

I shifted on the trunk and thought about putting my phone away, looking at my suit for the first time. The blood was all over my shirt and coat and turning brown as it dried. I wasn't excited to answer Kemble. Not just because that meant going over watching someone die, but because I had to tell him... and her... everything. It didn't take a lawyer to know that client confidentiality didn't cover failure to report a crime.

I told them both everything. I told them about the Beverlys. Liza Borden, the girlfriend. Blake, the best friend. Derrick Sayles, a possible suspect. And all of the dead ends that I had bumped into. I would glance at Ito, trying to figure out how mad she was going to be, but I couldn't read her. Which made it all the more frustrating.

When I was done, Kemble's head bent to the side. "Crap. A kidnapping. This means I gotta call the feds." A head shake. "I hate the fucking feds. They always treat us like we're fucking idiots."

I chose not to pluck that low-hanging fruit.

Kemble kept going. "Did you notice anything we can use to ID them? Narrow it down? License plate? Make of the car?"

I described the car as best as I could — another dead end. I hadn't seen the plate in the dark, and there were a million cars that looked the same in L.A.

"It just happened so fast. Matty... he was..." I didn't want to tell them about the Adderall. They'd find out soon enough. "He tackled the guy. He fucked up."

"That's generally what gets people killed," said Kemble.

"I was trying to get the two separated. I took my eye off the car. One of them knocked me to the ground; I got disorientated for a few moments." Seconds? "The other guy must've come out of the back of the car. I didn't see."

"You know," said Kemble, "none of this needed to happen. If the Beverlys... or you... had called us." He raised his eyebrows, and I got a whole lot of vice principal energy.

I glanced over at Ito and mumbled, "Yeah." That choice was weighing heavily on me.

Kemble told Ito he was going to take a look at the scene. She watched him trudge over for a moment and then turned to me.

"When I said another time, I didn't mean so soon," she said.

"I was desperate to get your attention." I felt terrible

making that joke, but I couldn't help myself.

I was rewarded with a lip curl. "How are you?" she asked, nodding toward Matty.

I looked over my shoulder. The crime scene techs were done with Matty's body; they were putting him into the ambulance, zipped into a bag. In the end, that's how all of us will get carried out.

"I've never seen anyone die before," I replied.

"Came close a few times," she said. "I'm usually there after the fact."

"He got so quiet. He looked so scared."

Ito stepped up onto the bumper and sat next to me.

I asked her, "What am I supposed to do with my clothes?"

"Your clothes?"

I pointed to my suit. "I'm covered with evidence, aren't I?" Oh, God. Matty was all over me. I thought about throwing up.

She shook her head slowly. "It's not… it's not evidence we need. You can…" She thought about what to say next. "You can do whatever you want with the suit."

I imagined what my dry cleaner would say when he saw it. Uncomfortable, he'd probably try to make a joke. "Hey, what happened? You in a horror movie or something?" Yeah, Francisco, I was. And then he'd feel bad and I'd feel bad.

I couldn't throw it away. Someone would find it and wonder and then call the cops and it would be a whole thing.

LAWRENCE ALLAN

I wondered if I could burn it without setting Los Angeles on fire. It had been 35 days since the last one.

Ito said something to me.

"What?" I said, coming back to reality.

"Are you OK to drive home?" she repeated.

"I can go home?"

She nodded. "We'll have more question, but…" She put a hand on my leg. "Do you have anyone to talk to about this? Because this is fucked-up. It will fuck with you."

I chuckled. "I have a *lot* of people to talk to." I pointed to myself. "I've had a lot of experience dealing with trauma." Some of it in healthy ways. "I'll be… well, not fine. No one is fine. But. Yeah. I hear you." I paused. "I thought you were going to yell at me."

"Thought about it."

I couldn't help cracking a grin. "It was going to be epic, wasn't it?"

She agreed. "It was going to be a barn burner."

I could imagine.

Shit, were we having a *moment*? Is a crime scene the place to do that? I felt like a teenager, sitting out at night on the trunk of my car with the girl that I liked and…

Kemble shouted, "Ito!"

She looked back toward her partner and the moment passed.

"You got work to do, Violet," I said, letting it go. "I can

take care of myself."

"You sure?"

"I'm sure. Besides, Kemble is gonna start getting all jealous, you spending time with me."

"Fuck him," she said with a smile.

I mustered a shaky smile in return. She patted me on the thigh and hopped off the car. "See you around, Cooper." And she headed to meet up with her partner.

I slid off my trunk and got in my car. I glanced in the rear view mirror at the collection of men and women still working the scene, then plugged my bloody phone in and started Ani DiFanco's "Pulse" as I left the parking lot.

Heading east on the 101, traffic was the same. The usual slow motion with everyone hoping to just zip in and out, but with no place to go but straight. There were red lights in front of me, white lights heading in the opposite direction, but it felt flat and intangible, like in those old movies where the hero and the femme fatale ride in a car that's actually in the studio, traffic rear-projected behind them. I had to concentrate so I didn't crash into someone.

Back on Sunset, now heading a little west, a car pulled up next to me at a stoplight. Inside, were two young women dressed for a night on the town. Both of them were in sparkles, and the red light bounced off them like they were disco balls. They moved to a song. Smiling. About to have the time of their lives.

The passenger, a black-haired Latina, glanced over at me. She saw the blood on my shirt and suit. Did I have some on my face? Maybe. I didn't know. I could see her eyes faltering, thinking that her night was about to get strange. I smiled back in a reassuring way, and she decided that the blood wasn't blood but had to be something else, and her mind went right back to the good night that she and her friend were planning.

The power of the mind, y'all.

The light turned green, and I peeled out, as much as my Toyota could peel.

Twenty minutes later, at almost eleven o'clock, I was home, parked, and stepping out of my car. I looked at my place. Through the shades of my own bungalow, I could see Dad sitting on the couch, watching something on the TV.

I couldn't deal with him right now, I didn't want to explain, and I doubted whether I'd get what I really needed from that man. I turned and headed to Moe's place instead. I quietly knocked on the door. "Moe?"

I hoped he wasn't entertaining because I had already interrupted once before and, quite frankly, there's no reestablishing a mood when a man in bloody clothes shows up at your door.

But he wasn't and he opened the door. He gasped and his eyes went all over me. "Honey! Are you OK?"

"Not a scratch on me," I said dully.

He took me by the hand and pulled me in, closing the door behind.

"I'll get some bags. We'll throw all of this away." Moe was on it.

I started stripping off the suit, which felt like a banana peel as the blood had coagulated. He was there with a trash bag. I dropped in the suit and shirt. "Go take a shower," Moe said. "I'll get you something to wear."

I did as I was told — it was great not having to answer any questions — and took a long, hot shower. After I had gotten the bloodstains off my chest, I stood there under the showerhead a little longer.

I thought about who was going to call Matty's parents. I wondered if he still *had* parents. Would the cops call his agent? Should I call his agent? It would be in the paper in the morning.

Moe knocked on the bathroom door and opened it just enough to slip some clothes onto the counter. Then he was gone. Another ten minutes in the shower, and I was turning pink. I turned off the water, dried off, and slipped on the shorts and T-shirt Moe had provided. The T-shirt featured a buff man; the words above his flexed biceps announced he was a "Mali-dude."

I padded down the hall into his living room, where he handed me a cup of herbal tea.

"You don't have to talk about it if you don't want to."

I took a sip and sat down, pushing my hand through my still wet hair. I felt the tea warm my chest, and I told him everything.

# 20

AN HOUR OR so later, I was down the hall of my place, almost to my bedroom, ready to crash, when I heard my dad call out.

"Jimmy?" His voice was quiet, like he didn't want to disturb me.

I had snuck past him when I came home. Just like old times. I found him asleep on the couch. He must've fallen asleep watching a movie, and I turned off the TV during the rolling credits.

"You OK?" he asked. I could hear him moving and shifting on the couch, followed up with a cough or two.

"I'm good," I answered, hoping that would be enough so I could get some sleep. There were going to be a lot of questions tomorrow that I wasn't looking forward to answering. I was beginning to fray.

"What?" he repeated.

"I said" — now repeating myself — "I'm *good.*" Of course, I said it in a way that could be construed as the exact opposite of good.

"It's late. Where have you been?" he said, turning on a light and looking at me. He paused. "You weren't wearing that when you left."

My dad, a regular Sherlock Holmes.

I turned around and stepped into the living room. "No, I wasn't." I could see that he was about to ask what happened and I put up my hand to stop him. "It'll be in the papers in the morning. Things..." I didn't know how to say it, so I said, "Things didn't go as planned."

"What was the plan?"

"Jesus, Dad, I want to go to bed."

"Are you OK?"

"I just told you that I am."

"I'm your dad; I know when you're lying. What was supposed to happen?"

"No." I put up a finger and wagged it. "You do *not* get to do that."

He shrugged. "Do what?"

"Try to be my fucking father," I said, and I hoped it hurt. I hoped it really got to him. I know Moe wanted me to be a better man, deal with that weight around my neck, but I was tired of the bullshit.

He nodded. "Yeah. OK. I get that. I left. I'm the bad guy. But I'm here now."

"Oh, here we are again. 'You're here *now*.' Whoop-de-do. Father of the Year!"

"Hey. What's going on?" Paul looked around my place like he had stepped onto the wrong soundstage. "I thought we were cool."

"Agreeing to a meeting with game show producers makes us *partners*, not cool."

"I just asked what happened," he protested. "Why am I the bad guy?"

The ground fell away beneath me, so that only the living room wall was propping me up. "Because you *left*. You left, Paul. You were gone. That's why you're the bad guy."

He walked away from me and headed to the kitchenette, where he opened the fridge. "Why is there only water? Like who doesn't have milk? Or juice." He turned to me. "You could at least have orange juice. This is California after all."

I pushed farther into the room.

"What are you — who *cares* that I don't have juice?!"

He shoved the fridge closed and whirled around, already preparing to defend himself. "Look. Your mom and I, it was clear we didn't get along. We were a disaster together."

"Disasters are why people get divorced. But you left. You

disappeared."

He muttered something.

"*What*?"

Paul repeated himself. "Things were hard."

"Hard? Oh, yeah. I bet. I *only* struggled through a years-long drug spiral, destroying my career, burning bridges, almost dying, and, oh, yeah, having my father walk out in the middle of that. But, go ahead, you tell me about hard."

Suddenly, he was emboldened. "It was really hard watching you throw everything away." Oh, look. He had found someone to blame: me. "Everything we worked for... you just shit on it, man! And there was nothing I could do. So, yeah. I ran away. I own that."

I could barely breathe. "I was a kid. You were supposed to be responsible for me."

He snorted. "I *was*. OK? I made sure you ate; I made sure you went to bed on time." He pointed at me. "I helped you with your lines; I took you to auditions; I was there every day on set with you."

I wanted to throw up. He really didn't know. Or he was so up his own ass he couldn't admit it.

"You don't know what happened to me, do you?"

He blinked, not answering.

"It was the movie in Seattle. The one where you pawned me off on Mike, the AD. Remember him?"

The movie in question was *Doug's in Love*, a dumb

romantic comedy aimed at adults. It was also PG-13, so the producers hoped it'd be a four-quadrant film, drawing in as many audience demos as possible. They were even shooting it in Seattle to cash in on people's nostalgia for *Sleepless in Seattle.* I was going to be number seven on the call sheet, my highest place yet. That put me behind the leads and some kids with bigger resumes than me in importance. Mom had the firm to worry about, so that meant it was up to Paul to take me. And, you know, be responsible for me.

"I didn't pawn you off on anyone," he protested.

This, of course, wasn't true, though it also didn't mean Paul Cooper was lying. It wasn't uncommon for him to take my jobs as an opportunity for himself to schmooze with the crew, especially the directors and the producers, in hopes of reigniting his career.

*Doug's In Love* was a big opportunity. I had three great scenes and I knew I could shine. And it would give him a chance to run elbows with some of the big names in comedy. If he couldn't be an action star, maybe he could be funny.

"You were thirteen. You didn't need — and you didn't want — me hovering around you."

"At thirteen I was still a kid. Surrounded by adults. I shouldn't have been the one making the decision to be left alone."

It was at costume fitting that Paul introduced me to Mike. Mike was in his late twenties, maybe early thirties, as tall as my dad, with hair that was beginning to thin. Mike seemed like he had his shit together. As first AD, it was his job to know where everyone needed to be, to get them there, and he did it with an easy-going smile. He was going to be the guy to take care of me.

Paul shook his head. "Well, I'm *so* sorry I left you alone on a big Hollywood set making a movie! Wow. Such a villain, letting you live out your dream." His sarcasm chilled me.

Maybe if I laid it out for him, he would finally see what he had done wrong. "You would drop me off at set and disappear, telling me that you'd see me back at the hotel. I would be alone, with Mike, all day long." Paul tried to interrupt, but I kept going. "He said everything right. So I would trust him. So I would depend on him. Because he was there. And I believed him."

I could see Paul pulling back, getting afraid, but I pressed on. "The days on set were fine. I had lots to do. But it was at night, at the hotel, when you didn't come back... those were hard. Those were lonely. Mike knew that."

Paul shook his head. It was clear he wanted to be anywhere else but right there in my living room.

"He's the one that gave me my first beer. Did you know that?" I nodded. "He told me how he totally got what I was going through. He called himself the original latchkey kid. His parents had gone through a nasty divorce and he would come home to an empty apartment. 'And you know what made things feel better?'" I mimicked Mike's smooth, sure voice. "How about an ice cold beer, Jimmy?"

It was the lizard in my brain that had said yes.

Paul put up his hand. "OK. Enough."

I pulled an innocent face. "Oh, I'm sorry. Is it *hard* to hear about? Because I haven't even gotten to the worst parts."

Like what Mike did to me.

Like how the next day he made me promise not to tell anyone and I was so scared and confused.

Like how, on the worst day of my life, I did the thing that made me famous.

This dumb movie where Paul Cooper let me down was about this guy named Doug who has fallen in love with a woman. His nephew — played by a moderately successful child actor — hated the new romance because that meant Doug wouldn't have any more time for him. So, us kids were going to destroy the relationship. Hi-larious.

"Listen, Jimmy..." Dad started.

But I told him. I told him about how the morning after Mike... Well, the morning after, I was on set. The director had walked us through the scene where the nephew explains his big plan, but I was spaced out, on another planet. I was keeping an eye on Mike. When it came time to shoot the scene, the cameras rolled, and the nephew did his bit, and then asked me, the best friend character, if I got it.

Without thinking, because I wasn't really there, I replied,

"Er.... Whaaaaat?"

Everyone laughed, and the director shouted, "Cut!"

Oh, no. Now I was in trouble. I was about to cry, but I couldn't because who was there — Mike? I knew the line, but couldn't say it. I was sure I would get fired, but instead the director said to me, "That was brilliant. *Perfect.* Can you do it again?"

And I did. Five more times until we got it. That "Er.... Whaaaaat?" became quotable. It became a thing. It became a *T-shirt.*

Funny how life is. Best and worst days on the exact same day.

"... I didn't know," said the man standing in my living room.

A week after that scene, Paul and I finally reconnected at the wrap party. And by reconnected, I mean we were both in the same place at the same time. He shook hands with the stars, gluing himself to the director, and claimed credit for my work. While he was doing that, the lizard in my brain suggested I steal and drink as many beers as I could, while trying to stay out of Mike's way.

Later that night, I threw up in the middle of our hotel room. Paul yelled at me, calling me selfish and stupid. He couldn't understand why I was being so difficult. Didn't I understand that I had a future?

Now he was standing in my house, shaking his head.

"Jimmy." He took a step closer. "I didn't know. I really didn't..." He paused and licked his lips. Telling the truth was hard for him.

I said, "It's not that you didn't *know* that hurts. It's that you didn't bother to find out why your kid was getting drunk and puking in hotel rooms. Why your kid was suddenly incredibly difficult to be around."

After a pause, he said dryly. "But you were *always* difficult to be around."

I couldn't help but snort. That was sort of funny. And well delivered. I laughed and so did he.

Then Paul Cooper, my dad, dropped his smile and looked down at the floor, taking a deep breath. He looked up at me, his eyes wet. "I'm really sorry I wasn't there, Jimmy. Like there there, you know? I was..." He looked for the word. "Selfish. And maybe I knew, but, with everything that was going on, I couldn't handle it." He shrugged. "I wasn't the guy you could rely on. I freaked out. I wasn't the father you and Erika needed." He pushed the back of his hand across his nose, sniffing. Dad shook his head and did his best to smile. "I'm really sorry that happened to you."

My fingers uncurled, and I was no longer a scared kid on a soundstage in Seattle. I was a grown and damaged man, back in my living room, shocked and surprised at what his father had said.

# 21

---

THE FBI WERE involved in the Beverly case now. Good times.

"The police should do all their interrogations up here. The view's fantastic." I stood at the window of a conference room, looking down and over Grand Park in downtown L.A. It was a weekend crowd down there, and by crowd, I mean the few people who lived downtown hanging out in the sun. A couple of guys tossed a Frisbee around.

"You're not being interrogated," said Erika as she stared at her phone, sitting on the opposite side of the conference table, facing the window. In front of her was a yellow legal pad and pen that she had pulled from her briefcase. "You're a witness."

Violet had called in the morning, inviting me to her precinct so the FBI could question me. She had also said that I was just a witness. When she hung up, I called Erika.

I looked at my sister and said, "Didn't Mom always say, 'Any time you're questioned by authorities, it's an interrogation'?"

"She's not wrong." Erika rolled her eyes from her phone to me. "I hope you didn't say that to your girlfriend."

"I didn't. And she isn't."

Erika hummed and returned to her phone.

Unsurprisingly, the morning after my talk with Dad had been pretty weird. Both of us pretended like nothing extraordinary had happened, that I hadn't confessed to sustaining a terrible trauma, much less that he had admitted to his tragic failures. But something had shifted between the two of us. He even tried making coffee, which, I guess, was his way of trying to make up for all of it.

I folded my arms, impatient. "And what's more important than my pending interrogation by the FBI?" I asked, nodding at her phone.

"You being in the *L.A. Times*."

I scooted closer, curious to know what they were saying about me. Old habits do not die. I reached for the phone, and she surrendered it.

The headline read: "Beloved Disney Star Murdered."

Below it, in smaller, yet still bold(ish) type: "Former Child

Star Witness."

I handed the phone back. "I'm not beloved? I'm former, and he's beloved?"

"He's dead, Jimmy," she said, head cocked, trying to bring me back to reality.

It's funny how death can reform someone the city had mostly forgotten into a "beloved star." For a hot second I wondered if that would happen to me. My time in the sun had been a little more complicated than Matty's, but no less worthy of respect when the time came.

Erika was still focused on the contents of the article. "It does ask some uncomfortable questions. Like wondering why two actors were involved in a kidnapping."

"We weren't involved." And technically, neither one of us were actors.

She looked at me, lips squished together.

"Not *involved* involved," I said to her glare. "Yes, we were both *involved* in the sense we were there to give money to the kidnappers, but..." I frowned. "Are they suggesting that I'm one of the kidnappers?"

"They aren't," she assured me. "But they are suggesting you're in over your head."

The door opened, and two Black women came in, dressed in FBI regulation suits.

"Mr. Cooper," said the taller of the two, "I'm Agent Alexander." In charcoal gray with a white shirt and a visitor's badge. Agent Alexander had short hair, large eyes, and a hand on her hip, opening her coat enough to reveal that she was armed. She gestured to her left. "This is Agent Martinez."

Martinez, a little lighter in skin tone, had hair that barely brushed her shoulders. She wore black and carried a large, thick folder.

Erika stood a little and offered her hand. "I'm Erika Cooper." Alexander and Martinez moved down to their side of the table and shook her hand. "I represent Mr. Cooper."

Alexander marked that. "Oh, a family affair." As I sat down next to my sister, she raised an eyebrow and said to me, "Do you think you need a lawyer, Mr. Cooper?" She had a bit of a Texan drawl.

I shrugged. "I like to bring a lawyer everywhere I go. Keeps me out of trouble."

No smiles, no reaction.

Erika sighed.

This was going *great*.

"Where's Vi — uh, Detective Ito?"

Martinez opened the file and pulled out a recorder. "She's not needed for this."

Alexander leaned back, lacing her fingers together. "Shall we start? We're going to record, if you have no objections."

Erika shook her head.

"People always told me I have a great voice," I supplied.

"That I should've done animation work."

The agents looked at me. They did not care for my brand of bullshit banter. I smiled.

Alexander carried on with her job. "Mr. Cooper, when were you engaged by the Beverlys?"

"Last Sunday. They told me their son had been kidnapped. They wanted me to find him before the exchange."

"Why didn't they contact the authorities?" asked Alexander.

I shifted in my seat. Erika looked at me. I answered. "I told them that's what they should do."

"But why didn't they?"

I shrugged. "Rich people."

Alexander leaned forward. "That's a pretty flip answer."

"I thought he was just a witness," stated Erika.

"I'm not trying to be flip." I shrugged. "As rich people, the Beverlys feel they live by different rules. Or maybe that the rules don't apply to them. I don't know. But they felt the safest way to get their son back was to not go to the police. They were afraid that someone would leak the news and..."

Alexander nodded. Martinez scribbled something down.

"And how did you come to work for the Beverlys?"

"Huh?"

"Why you?" she clarified.

"Why not me?" I replied, even though, yeah, I still had the same question.

Martinez sighed. "I thought you weren't going to be flip?" She spoke with just a bit of NYC. I wondered if she was struggling in L.A. with all its good weather and hiking possibilities.

"And I thought he was just a witness," Erika started again. "Because this feels very much like an interrogation."

Alexander put her hand up. "We currently believe that Mr. Cooper has been a witness to a crime."

"Currently" was doing a lot of heavy lifting in that sentence.

She continued. "What do you know about Edward Stratton?"

I paused and chewed my lip. Why were they asking about him? "He's the Beverlys' security guy."

Martinez and Alexander nodded but said nothing, which meant I had to keep talking.

"I only met him once. Twice. Right, he was there at the Beverlys' yesterday. I don't know... he was weird."

"Weird?" asked Martinez. "Weird how?"

"Yeah. Like, for a guy who recommended me..." Something clicked. "You're interested in Stratton." I leaned forward. "Do you think he did it? Oh, man. That would be..." Something else clicked. "Wait. You wanted to know why me. You think it's suspicious that he recommended me for the job, don't you?"

"Well..." started Martinez.

"Not to be...mean about it," said Alexander, "but there are professionals, even private ones, who are better equipped for this sort of thing than you are."

I smacked the table. "I was saying the same thing to Matty!"

Erika cleared her throat. Right, this wasn't actually about me.

"I'm not working with Stratton," I said, eyes wide. "I want that to be clear."

Alexander shook her head. "We don't think you're in on it."

"Just useful," offered Martinez.

My face flushed. I knew where she was heading. It never feels good to be the useful idiot. And if it was true, it also explained why Matty was brought on board. Stratton didn't want us to find Patrick, so he suggested the two of us bumbling Dr. Watsons for the job.

In doing so, Stratton ended up putting a target on Matty's back.

"What's Stratton saying?" asked Erika.

Silence. Alexander was making a decision.

"He's in the wind," she settled on. "Since last night. The Beverlys got your client's call " — she meant me, the call I'd made from the Park and Ride lot — "Stratton was gone from their home before the police arrived."

Obviously that was a big, red flag of suspicion. I had

moved from shame to anger. I was feeling stupid for not seeing it. Matty was dead because I didn't see it.

Erika said, "He's your prime suspect?"

Alexander had been studying my reactions but now looked over at my sister. "He's definitely a person of interest. And he would have to be working with at least one other person...."

"But we're looking at all the options," added Martinez. "Are there any other options?" she asked me.

"What?" I was a million miles away. I shook my head, trying to come back. "Yeah, yeah."

I took a deep breath and went through my week. I told them about Patrick and his attempts at real estate deals and how that led me to Derrick Sayles, who arguably had a motive. I described my meetings with people on my list and how it all came to nothing. Which, if Stratton was using me, made a whole lot of sense. "I'll send you my files."

"Let's talk about last night," said Alexander.

Goody.

I went over it again for the feds. It felt rehearsed now. It didn't quite rub me raw anymore. I went over the setup. How Matty behaved. That I suspected he was on something. I guess he wanted to feel, I don't know, strong, but he was all hyped up, and he was the cause in some ways of his own death. If he had just —

They weren't interested in that. They wanted me to focus

instead on the voice and demeanor of the kidnapper. His voice was deep, but he was putting it on. He was confident. He was used to these sorts of situations.

I described how Matty lost control —

And Alexander again asked me to focus on the man who stabbed Matty. What could I tell her? What did I see?

I paused, remembering something. "The first guy, he was... saying something. Over and over." I closed my eyes. "He was cursing, 'Oh, shit! Oh, shit.' He was surprised. Like he wasn't prepared for the other guy to... you know... stab someone."

Martinez almost nodded, but caught herself. I was onto something, I guess.

"Do you have any more questions?" asked Erika.

Alexander shook her head. "Not at this time, but we'll call you if we do." They stood. Martinez closed the file and snatched the recorder, turning it off.

I wasn't ready for the meeting to be over. I had questions of my own.

"Why him?"

The agents looked at me.

"Why is Stratton doing this? I would guess that working for the Beverlys is a good gig. So, why him? Why now?"

Alexander gave a wry smile. "All great questions. Which we'll ask when we find him."

"I was thinking we could — "

She interrupted me. "There is literally no 'we.' This is now our case. Go back to work. Or go home. Watch a movie. Whatever." Her smile thinned. "Thank you for your help."

And with that, they swept out of the room.

Two minutes later, Erika and I were in the elevator heading down. I leaned against the wall, watching the numbers tick by.

Adjusting her shoulder bag, Erika said, "That wasn't so bad."

I glanced at her.

"You're not a suspect," she offered, shrugging.

"Sure, not a suspect. Just an idiot."

"Would you rather be a suspect?"

I turned to her, snapping, "Actually, *yeah*." I went back to staring at the numbers. As a suspect, I'd at least have been taken seriously.

The elevator dinged, and the door opened onto the marbled first floor. Cops, robbers, and their lawyers headed in various directions after passing through security. Erika and I stepped out and to my right, I spotted Violet Ito with Kemble, both of them talking to an older man with a scowl on his face. I've seen those sorts of scowls before from studio execs and producers — the in-charge type. They're the bosses that want to tell you how to do your job even though they haven't done it in years. I caught Ito's eye and was about to step closer when she shook her head, warning me off.

I changed course, and Erika and I headed out the front door. Which was a mistake.

Because that's where we ran into the press.

Reporters immediately started shouting questions as they all raised their cameras, and it was like a wave of noise and humanity crashing toward me and my sister. In an instant, Erika grew three inches taller, her voice dropped, and she was my hero. "We are not answering any questions today," she said with final authority.

The reporters groaned.

I leaned to her ear and whispered, "Not even one?"

Her glare was enough.

"Sorry, y'all," I shouted. "We'll have to do this another time."

Someone yelled, "What was Matty Goodman doing there? Are there any suspects?"

Erika pulled at me before I could open my mouth. She wedged through the crowd, pulling me along in her wake. The questions kept coming.

"Do you feel responsible for Matty's death?"

"Were you with him when he died?"

"What were Matty's last words?"

"Have you talked to his mother yet?"

I turned and looked at the bearded asshole who was holding up his phone, filming the whole thing.

Mumbling, I said, "I didn't know he had a mother."

Erika jerked, and I stumbled away from the mess. We walked quickly so that only the most energetic of the reporters kept up with us. Eventually, though, once they knew I wasn't going to give them anything, they gave up and fell away.

After a couple of blocks, we went into a parking garage and up a couple of levels. We walked to Erika's car, and she beeped it unlocked. "What are you thinking about?" she asked me. She opened the back driver's side door and dropped her bag on the back seat.

"Hm?"

"You haven't said anything in five minutes. That makes me worried."

I sighed. "Matty's mom."

Her cheeks puffed as she blew out air. She took my hand. "It must've been scary."

"You have no idea, Erika."

She squeezed my hand.

"I also told Dad."

"Told him what?"

I looked away, and then up at the ceiling of the parking garage. Then to her. "About what happened to me. About the AD in Seattle."

She went pale. "Oh, shit. You did? And? How did... how are you?"

How was I? That was a good question. I looked away again, hoping the answer would come. It was sort of peaceful in this parking garage. Ideal for getting answers from the universe. No traffic. No helicopters. Just the breeze. "I'm good."

Not all revelations are equal, I guess.

"OK. I you want to talk more...?" she offered.

I shook my head.

She gave me a hug and put a hand to my cheek. "Call me if you need to."

"Of course."

Erika got into her car and started it up. She rolled down the window.

"You're going home, right?" she asked. "You're going to listen to what Agent Alexander said?"

I shrugged. "She *really* meant what she said, Erika."

She stared at me. "She really did, Jimmy."

"I could hear it in her voice."

Erika shifted in her seat, unsure if she should get out and slug me or not. She chose peace. She put the car in reverse and started pulling away. I turned, heading to my car. Erika stopped and rolled down her window. She stuck her head out and said, "Just don't do anything stupid."

# 22

GORDON BIXBY CALLED me that afternoon.

I was parked across the street from the Beverly estate, "Another Girl, Another Planet," playing on my stereo, watching the comings and goings of the FBI. There were two black SUVs when I got there, and two more had arrived after. The drivers and front seat passengers wore those Bureau windbreakers with the Bureau sunglasses. They liked to roll hard, just like in the movies. Perks of the job, I guess.

I made a face, hesitating to answer the call. This was going to be embarrassing, but, I couldn't not answer. I poked my phone. "Gordon! Hey, how — "

"What the hell am I reading?" he barked.

"Saw the *Times* article, huh?"

"Uh-huh." Gordon wasn't happy. He had always much preferred to emphasize the "private" in private detective. He and Mom had crazy notions that I couldn't do my job if I was recognized everywhere. Joke's on them... right?

"Yeah, not one of my finer moments, Gordon."

"Jesus, no." He cleared his throat.

I shook my head, agreeing with him.

"You OK?" he said.

I took a long, slow breath. "I'm not great. Watched someone get stabbed. Didn't sleep well. Questioned by the FBI. I might be someone's useful idiot. Oh, and my dad is staying with me."

"Oh. I didn't know. How's that working out?"

I gave a slight shrug. "Not as terrible as you would've thought." I sighed. "We might even be... all right."

Gordon didn't say anything. He had only met my dad once or twice before he disappeared, and that was long before Gordon and I worked together. But I don't think he liked him very much.

Finally he said, "You got a plan?"

"Oh, uh..." There was movement at the front door. Agents were stepping out of the house, including one that looked like Agent Alexander. They climbed into one of the SUVs, which left soon after.

"You don't have a plan," he said with a sigh, finishing my thought.

"Have I ever been a plan sort of guy?"

"This is why I retired. You made things too exciting."

I grinned.

Gordon continued, saying, "Just don't go stumbling through this, OK?"

"I wouldn't be me if there wasn't a little stumbling."

He didn't take the bait and laugh. Not even a chuckle. "Jimmy, you owe it to that kid to do it right."

I licked my lips. My voice quiet, I said, "Yeah, I know." I took a breath. "I got this. OK? You'll be proud of me."

"Of course I will."

I looked at the house. "Gordon, I gotta — "

"Go. Yeah. Of course. Go get the bad guys."

I clutched the phone for a second after we disconnected. It was good to hear his voice. Gordon Bixby wasn't known for emotional displays; he was more of a man of action and deed. Even though we didn't agree on how to do something, it meant a lot that he showed up.

I slipped the phone into my suit coat, crossed the street, and waved to the guard at the gate with my best "Hey, you know me" grin. It wasn't necessarily wrong or illegal talking to the Beverlys. After all, they were technically still my clients. They hired me to find their son and he was still out there. And now, I wanted to know a little more about Edward Stratton.

I got to the porch and straightened my tie. Always look

your best. I was about to ring the bell when the front door opened.

Mr. Beverly was there, looking exhausted in a Pima cotton robe. His eyes were deep-set, and his face wrinkled. One look at me and his face narrowed. "You dumb fuck."

I looked back at the guardhouse just in time to see the guard hang up the phone. Well, I guess I had been expected. "Mr. Beverly, I'm sorry — "

A finger wedged its way into my face. "You could have gotten my son *killed.*"

As if someone else hadn't been. Prick.

He stepped onto the stoop. "You're lucky I don't strangle you."

I put up a hand, as if that was going to be an actual defense. "With all due respect, I had suggested — "

"You had *one* job: find my son. He could be dead now for all I know."

There was a pretty good chance that I was, indeed, fired.

Two men appeared in the doorway behind him, FBI agents in those windbreakers, a Latino guy and a white guy in their thirties. The white guy had a mug of coffee in his hand. "Is there a problem, Mr. Beverly?" he asked.

Mr. Beverly was shaking with rage. "Yes, there's a goddamn problem. There's some fucking trash on my doorstep."

The Latino agent took a step outside the house. "Sir," he told me, "I'm going to have to ask you to leave."

That wasn't enough for Richie Rich. "Don't ask him to *leave*. Take him in. Do *something*!" shouted Mr. Beverly. "He fucked us."

That was all I could take. I had eaten enough shit.

"You fucked us, asshole!" I shot back. "You wanted to keep things under wraps. I told you to go to the police. And in the end, *who* was the bad guy? It was Edward, the guy *you* hired."

Beverly charged at me, and the agents moved swiftly, getting in between us.

The agent looked at me again. "You really need to leave."

I put up my hands. "I want the same thing everyone wants. I want to find Patrick. I just want to ask Mr. Beverly some questions about Edward Stratton."

"I'm not going to say it again," the agent stated in an even voice.

Taking the hint, I turned on my heel and walked back down the driveway and past the guard, who smugly looked at me. Mr. Beverly was ushered back inside.

As I crossed the street, my phone rang. I dug it out and snapped, "Yeah?"

"Mr. Cooper, I'm sorry for my husband's behavior."

I stopped in front of my car and looked back at the mansion. On the second floor, I saw a curtain flutter as someone left the window. "Mrs. Beverly?" I was certain that had been Patrick's room.

"You have to understand," Eva began, "he loves Patrick very much."

I nodded.

"My husband is also very serious, though. I don't think you should be standing in the street in front of our house."

I started moving again, getting into my car. "I'm sorry I couldn't get Patrick last night."

"I understand. It turns out you never had a chance." She paused. "I'm sorry about what happened to your friend."

My friend? I didn't correct her.

"Did the FBI tell you anything?'

She took a deep breath. "They asked a lot of questions about Edward. Can you believe it? We trusted that man."

Silence. Betrayal took time to process.

"Do you think he will hurt Patrick?"

I wasn't sure what to tell her.

"Mr. Cooper?" Her voice was breathless.

I told her the truth. "I don't know. Patrick was the thing they wanted to trade for money. They got the money, but..." Then I lied. "I'm sure he'll be fine."

They just might hurt him, is all.

She was quiet for a long while. "Edward was the one that suggested we didn't need to go to the police. Robert didn't put up much of a fight. I don't blame him for that. He had a rather awful time when he was younger. He was always in the newspaper. Always being talked about." Her voice shuddered.

"Why do you think Edward would do this?" I asked her. "Was he hurting for money?"

"I don't know. He shouldn't have been."

Out my window on both sides of the street were a long line of mansions, running down a hill. The Beverly estate sat at the top; and everything else was below.

She went on. "Ever since he was hired five years ago, Edward has always been trusted. We put our safety in his hands. Maybe he had grown unhappy. He had started to... It felt like he was pulling away."

I sat up. "When did you notice that?"

"A few months ago. Normally he paid such attention to detail, but he had started delegating. Things were just... sloppy. Very unlike him."

I nodded and chewed my bottom lip. Something had happened to Stratton a few months ago. Something that made him need a lot of money.

I said, "And he never came to you or Robert, asking for money or... for help for anything?"

"Not that I'm aware of." Her voice was soft. Caring.

"Mrs. Beverly, I'm sorry about last night. I'm still determined to get Patrick home safe and sound." I stopped. "But, just so you know, it's probably unwise for you to mention to anyone that..."

"You're still working the case?"

"I don't want to get you into trouble."

After a moment, she said, "I'll tell my husband and the FBI that I told you in no uncertain terms to stay the hell away from my son."

"Perfect, thanks."

She hung up.

# 23

MAYBE EDWARD STRATTON owed someone a lot of money and kidnapping Patrick was the only way he could get it.

I was driving east on Sunset Boulevard, heading home, listening to "Valerie Loves Me" by Material Issue and doing some thinking. Sunset isn't the fastest way to get across the city, but it tells a story and I appreciate that. It bobs and weaves, cutting through rich and middle class neighborhoods, past the northern edge of UCLA, before arriving into West Hollywood and then carrying on without me.

But then, how does a guy like Edward owe anyone *that much* money? Once upon a time, I owed people a bunch of money. They would never have allowed me to get that deep into debt. They would've broken more than my legs.

Then maybe he just got tired of being an employee of the One Percent and wanted a taste of the very good life. Edward Stratton would be quite the big fucking deal with that much money on hand.

I put it out of my mind. His motive wasn't all that important. The FBI were looking for him. Once they got him, then his motive would come out. At the moment, Patrick still had to be found. And I wasn't sure where to start.

The sun was setting when I got home.

"Good news," said Dad as I stepped into my place. "I talked the producers down." He was very pleased with himself.

I frowned and pulled at my tie. "Talked them down from what?" I slipped out of my coat and dropped it on the back of the couch as I headed to the fridge.

"Out of going in another direction," he answered.

I turned around. "Another direction?" That was Hollywood speak for, We're firing you, but we don't want to call it a firing because maybe someday we will want to hire you back. "They were going to go — "

Dad put up a hand. "They're not."

"Why were they?"

His hands circled in the air as he tried to figure out how to explain. "It's the whole thing that happened last night. The..." He lost a little color in his face.

He didn't want to mention Matty's death.

"The...?"

He was also trying to avoid mentioning my failure to get Patrick back.

"They didn't think it would be a good look for the show. But!" He put up his hand. "I explained it to them."

I took a breath. Oh, boy. "What did you explain to them?"

"I told them, 'You wanted Jimmy Cooper. And Jimmy Cooper is now a private detective.' And then I spun it, you know…. 'There's a bit of danger, an edge, an *excitement* when you have Jimmy Cooper on your show.' Because of your job, people are going to talk about you."

My phone dinged in my coat pocket. I stepped over to grab it, saying, "You know, Dad, that… that's great. I'm really impressed."

He beamed. "You just have to know how to talk to these guys. They're always so worried. You've got to make them feel like everything is going to be OK."

It was nice seeing him like this. Capable.

I looked at the text on my phone. It was from an unknown number and said: *Outside, now, D.*

D? Danny.

Dad must have seen the look on my face because he asked, "What's going on?"

I peeked through the blinds of my bungalow's front window. I didn't see anyone standing out there. My phone dinged again.

*We need to talk.*

I puffed out some air and turned to Dad. "OK. Uh. I need to talk with someone, and I need you to stay here."

He knotted his brow. "What's going on?" he said again.

I rolled up my sleeves. "Just need to chat with someone."

"Jimmy, you're making me nervous."

My hand on my doorknob, I gave my best reassuring smile. "Nothing to worry about. An old friend." I opened the door and stepped out. I leaned back in. "Just... lock the door behind me." Closing it, I moved outside.

I looked around for Danny, but I didn't see anyone. Then a car flashed its headlights across the street. With a deep breath, I jogged across. As I got closer, I didn't recognize the tough guy in the driver's seat. He seemed both laid back and not to be fucked with as he pointed to the backseat.

The window rolled down, and there was Danny.

Danny had gained some weight since I had last seen him. He was now shaving his head, so that the dark skin of his scalp glinted in the streetlight. "Get in," he said.

It was not a suggestion. I got in.

Danny shifted so his back was against the door and he was facing me. He didn't look pleased. "You told me the cops weren't involved," he said.

I nervously laughed. "At the time that I talked to you, that was totally true."

He did not find it amusing. "I want to be able to trust you, Jimmy."

"I want that too," I said. "Things didn't go well."

He shook his head. "I read the papers. The Feds are involved."

"They are."

Danny nodded. "On a scale of importance, there's the LAPD" — he put his hand at the level of his chest — "and then there's the FBI." He moved his hand to his head. "I don't like this kind of attention."

Oh, shit. What had I gotten myself into? I put up my own hands. "And no one is giving it to *you*. The feds aren't interested in me. The cops are not interested in me. I'm just a *witness*."

"Uh-huh."

Danny looked over his shoulder, back at my place.

My father was looking through the blinds.

"Who's that?"

Another nervous laugh. "That's my dad." I wondered if this was going to be the last time Dad saw me. Then I realized he would make himself the hero in the story of *my* disappearance.

Danny looked at me. "No shit, your dad?" he said, surprised. "He came back?"

"Yeah."

He observed my dad for a second. "Fucking hell. He came back." He shook his head. "After all the shit you told me about back in the day, I would never have guessed that."

I leaned forward. If I kept Danny talking, maybe I could talk him out of whatever he had in store for me. "The weird thing is — "

My movement caught the eye of the driver and I leaned back. Maybe not.

"Weird thing is, we're, like, in a good place," I said.

Danny raised an eyebrow. "Seriously?"

"A healing place. Step by step. But, yeah. He's back." I gave him a nervous smile.

Danny's mouth curled and he nodded. "Well. All right then." His demeanor changed. It was all business again. "I got you a name."

He had my attention. I guess I wasn't in trouble. And possibly I had a way to find Edward on my own. "You're still wanting to help, even with the heat?"

Danny paused. "*Teenage Life of Riley* was fire. If you can get the fuck that killed Matty, I'm happy to help."

Hey. Criminals watch TV too. They can be fans. Don't judge.

"This fence, he's important. A lot of people in L.A. use his services." Danny folded his hands together. "And those people would be very unhappy if something were to happen to him."

"I feel like you're telling me that I shouldn't let this guy get swept up in any sort of thing."

Danny pointed a finger at me. "Now you're getting it. I

was never here," he cautioned me. "Never call me again."

I had one foot already out of the car as I said, "I thought I owed you."

"Get the guy, and we're even."

# 24

THE FENCE'S NOM de plume was Ray-Ray. A powerful statement from a white guy who grew up in Woodland Hills, a quaint little neighborhood in the northwest part of L.A. Ray-Ray had been a part of the underworld for decades, and over time, he had become more and more important to the criminal ecosystem. After all, someone had to turn ill-gotten gains into cold hard cash. If that was you, and you could find him, Ray-Ray was your man.

He had a stylish, modern mini-mansion in Sherman Oaks, just on the north side of the Hollywood Hills. Don't believe what they say, kids; crime does pay. Looking at the cars in his driveway, the house, and the Gucci sunglasses and the thousand_dollar tracksuit he wore, Ray-Ray was paid quite well for his services.

I had been following him from his mini-mansion all around the area since Sunday afternoon. In his forties, Ray-Ray kept his hair short and his beard immaculately trimmed. His gold pinky ring was a statement, as was the large phone he was always on. Even while he drove. Dude was one distraction away from an accident.

It was now late Monday morning, and Ray-Ray was having brunch at a place on Ventura Boulevard, eating out front. While I watched him wolf down some waffles, I listened to LP croon "The One That You Love." What a voice.

My hope was if Ray-Ray was the fence, he hadn't met with Stratton yet. I wasn't expecting a big exchange. Ray-Ray wasn't sitting on tens of millions of dollars, and he wasn't going to collect fifty mil just because some guy said he had the goods. Unsurprisingly, criminals didn't always trust one another.

I had learned that the hard way when I was still doing movies. It was between a teen comedy called *Love Is Blind* — yes, the hook has aged really poorly — and the creature feature I did, *Vampire Empire*. I was at the point of my addiction that I was still calling it a good time. I was already starting to run out of doctors who would give me pills without too many questions, and I had already tapped out my friends.

Which meant I had to go to less-than-legal sources. That

might've been a red flag for some, but, like I said, I was still having a good time and therefore always looking for the next *great* time. Which meant I wound up in places like the apartment in Ladera Heights giving some guy named Two Times — for reasons that no one explained — $300 in cash. He handed me a baggie of pills and wished me a good night.

When I got back to my place in West Hollywood and started popping them I noticed I didn't feel a thing. Zilch. Nada. I took a few more and still nothing. No good times. No warm ,fuzzy feeling like slipping into a warm bath.

Frustrated, I really looked at them. I couldn't be sure, but I suspected they were just fucking aspirin.

I was lucky it wasn't something else and I didn't overdose.

But I was pissed.

I drove back south to Ladera Heights, you know, to speak with the manager. Two large men at the bottom of the stairs dissuaded me from doing that. I took the hint and drove back home.

I did hear about Two Times about a year later. He turned up dead in a parking lot in Torrance. I guess he pulled his stunt too many times.

As I broke out of the memory, I saw that Ray-Ray was on the move. After brunch, he headed west on Ventura and ended up turning into the parking garage of the Sherman Oaks Galleria, a sort of indoor/outdoor mall. He went all the way to the top and backed into a spot away from the elevator banks, which got me excited.

He wasn't here to shop. He was here to meet someone.

I parked closer to the elevators, but still with a view of Ray-Ray's Benz.

A twenty-something white guy headed over. The guy was in good shape, wearing basketball shorts and a Lakers tank, a casual outfit for a day at the mall. He nodded slightly to Ray-Ray and got into the passenger seat.

Who was this guy? He wasn't Stratton. Was this guy here to fence something else? It was one of those times it would've been super helpful to have those listening devices like they have on TV. You know, one of those long-range microphone things that allow for eavesdropping.

Ten minutes later, the guy got out of the car and shoved the door closed. He winced and grabbed his shoulder, but he hadn't hurt himself closing the door. And then it occurred to me: maybe he hurt his shoulder when a certain former child star tackled him to the ground.

Ray-Ray started his car and pulled out of his spot. I had a choice. Follow Ray-Ray until he actually took a meeting with Edward Stratton or follow this guy.

I chose this guy.

Ray-Ray's Benz went by my car as I ducked down, hoping he didn't see me. I didn't need anything to go wrong.

The younger guy headed to the other side of the upper deck, and I kept low, watching. He kept rubbing his shoulder.

Edward, of course, was going to lay low. He had people looking specifically for him. He couldn't just make a run to the mall. There were too many cameras around for that.

A blue Volkswagen Jetta backed out of a spot with the Lakers guy at the wheel. I started my car but didn't move. He passed me and headed down the ramp; I pulled out and followed. Leaving the garage, he went north, and then turned onto Magnolia Boulevard and headed east.

Twenty minutes later, we ended up in Valley Village, a neighborhood just west of North Hollywood. He pulled into the driveway of a two story-house while I passed on by, finding parking a few doors down. It was a quiet, tree-lined, suburban street. It sort of reminded me of Haddonfield, Illinois, in *Halloween*. The original, not the remake. The stretch of houses just seemed too normal to be safe.

# 25

___

I WAITED UNTIL the sun set and the streetlights started coming on. I hadn't seen any movement, which made me worry that maybe I had followed the wrong guy. Maybe Ray-Ray did meet with Edward Stratton somewhere else, and now he was flying to some faraway destination, like the Philippines.

I couldn't shake the feeling I was right, though. That this was the guy that Matty fought. That this was maybe the place they were holding Patrick. I thought about calling Ito and telling her what I had found, but, what did I really have? A hunch? Ray-Ray might be known to the cops, but that didn't mean he was involved in this. And a hurt shoulder? The young guy could've hurt himself playing volley ball at

Venice Beach for all I knew.

I needed something more. Something that she could act on.

Climbing out of my car, I looked up and down the street. Quiet. Just like it would be right before Michael Myers jumps out of a tree and stabs you with a butcher knife.

(I guess that movie freaked me out more than I realized at ten years old. What was my dad thinking?)

I walked to the front of the house, a nice American Craftsman. The lights were on, but I didn't see any movement. There was a camera by the door, but I was guessing — hoping — no one was staring at a monitor. One last check of the street — no Michael Myers — and I headed up the driveway, to the left of the house.

Squeezing past the Jetta, I came to a window that looked into the dining room and the kitchen beyond. The light was also on here, but no one was there. I reached the back corner of the house and took a peek.

The driver of the car was out back, vaping and staring into his phone, his back to me. He took another drag and chuckled at something on the screen. I looked and saw a back door. I gritted my teeth and thought about making a bad decision. I really shouldn't, but I still had nothing.

With his back turned, I crept through the back door. I stepped into a family room by the looks of it. A pretty Spartan one. There was an IKEA couch and chair, a TV, and beyond that was the kitchen I had passed. To my left were stairs leading up. There was nothing distinctive about this place.

It was a rental. Maybe an Airbnb. But that's not a crime and I still couldn't call Ito.

I looked at the stairs, then back through the door. The guy was still vaping. I wondered where Edward was. Looking at the stairs again... *Well*, I thought, *in for a penny*.

I took them two at a time, on my toes, trying to be as quiet as possible. I had spent a lot of my youth sneaking home late at night, after some party or another, and for the most part I didn't get caught.

On the landing I looked around. One of the doors was closed, another was cracked open, and the third opened onto a bedroom that someone had been sleeping in. One could have Patrick behind it, or some innocent person who actually belonged here. And there was still no sign of Edward.

A toilet flushed. My heart thumped in my chest. I moved behind a corner on the landing.

The door opened, and out came Patrick, drying his hands on the front of his shirt. I'll forgive that unhygienic transgression, given the circumstances and the fact that my heart was thumping in my chest. I had him; the day could still be saved.

He spotted me and stopped moving. I put up a finger to shush him, then mouthed, "Where's the other kidnapper?"

He shook his head, confused.

I tried again. "Where's the *other* one?"

He shook his head again.

"The other — "

He got it. He pointed to the door that was cracked.

I nodded and waved him toward me.

He looked confused again. Kids these days.

"Come with me if you want to live," I said.

Patrick's eyes went wide. Clearly this kid hadn't see any of the Terminator movies.

"Come on," I mouthed.

Patrick walked closer to me, and I led the way down the stairs. At the bottom, I stopped him from going on. I moved closer to the back door and looked outside.

The guy was gone.

Shit, shit. I looked around the yard. He wasn't there! Where the fuck was he? Where —

Then I saw stars exploding in front of my eyes, and the world narrowed to a tunnel. I thought about throwing up, but instead I let gravity take hold of me. I fell to the floor, into blackness, as I muttered, "Not again."

---

AN ETERNITY LATER, someone was shaking me. Who the fuck was shaking me? It felt so good to lie on the floor. No obligations, no potential disappointment. Just some rest. I opened my eyes and slurred, "Stop it. Just stop."

It was Patrick; as he realized I was awake and responsive, his hands let go of my sport coat. He looked terrified. "We *have to go*," he whispered.

I wasn't sure why — the floor was so comfortable — but he pulled me up anyway. As I rose, I saw what had gotten him so nervous. On the floor, with a halo of red around his head, lay Edward Stratton.

"What happened?" I asked. "How long — ?"

Patrick pulled me out the back door. I glanced back at the family room. Everything was happening so fast. I also kept wondering if my head was actually that heavy.

Outside, we moved down the driveway. Patrick moved around the Jetta, but I didn't quite make it and banged my knee into the bumper. "*Ow*," I hissed. Stumbling, I still managed to stay on my feet.

At the sidewalk, Patrick stopped and asked, "Where did you park?"

I vaguely pointed down the street, digging for my keys. I aimed and beeped my car open. We moved in the direction of the light flash.

When we reached the car, Patrick said, "*That's* your car?"

Hey. What did he have against my car?

I put a hand on the roof to steady myself before opening the driver's-side door.

"Should you be driving?" I couldn't see his face well, but Patrick sounded concerned.

My eyes narrowed at the shadow I hoped was Patrick. "Well, yeah," I tried for cool and collected. "It *is* my car, after all." Like I was going to let him drive after he insulted my Toyota. Besides, I'd driven in worse conditions.

Spoilers: And in none of them should I have been driving.

I got in and looked back toward the house. It was hard to tell... Was someone coming out? Where was the other guy?

I wasn't going to stick around to find out. I slammed my door shut. Patrick got in on the other side, and I brought the car to life and floored the gas. The road waved back and forth like a crazy river, but I managed to navigate it.

I shook my head. Things were starting to come back into focus. The back of my skull felt like a big, throbbing mess. I touched it and found a glob of blood on my fingers.

"What happened?" I asked Patrick.

"Edward. It was Edward. He was downstairs. He hit you, and I was able to..." His voice broke. "Oh, God. Is he dead?"

Dead? Oh, boy.

"What about the other guy?" I barely paused at a stop sign before turning right.

Patrick shook his head, shrugged. He looked like a mess. He swallowed and said, "You were there, weren't you? When that guy got killed?"

I nodded. "Your parents hired me to find you." I pulled out

my phone and slowed — I didn't think anyone was following — and dialed a number.

Ito answered on the first ring. "Jimmy?"

"Heeeeeeeyyyy." I pulled over and looked around for a street sign. Where was I? "Good news. So don't be mad."

"What did you do, Jimmy?" she asked, slowly, clearly, and sounding very worried.

"I have Patrick Beverly. I found him." I looked at him, making sure he was still there. His head was resting against the window, staring out. "But. There might be a problem."

She said nothing for a long, hot second. "What sort of problem?"

"It was sort of a breakout," I explained. "There was a fight. One of them might be dead."

"Jesus, Jimmy."

"I said might. Probably."

"Probably or might?"

I paused. "I didn't check his *pulse*. We were in the middle of an escape. There was another guy."

"Where are you?"

I gave her the cross streets and the house's address.

She said, "I'll send units right now. When it's clear, I'll tell you. When that happens, I want you and Patrick back at the crime scene." Then she hung up.

Patrick had heard what she said and looked afraid. He was clearly not a fan of that idea. I put up a hand, trying to reassure him.

"We can't go back," said Patrick.

I shook my head. "The other guy's not going to stick around, especially not when he starts hearing sirens. It's going to be fine."

He wrapped his arms around himself and stared down at the dashboard.

It was quiet while we waited for her to call me back, and in the silence I kept looking at Patrick. I sort of didn't believe it. After all this, I was finally looking at him with my own eyes. It's funny how I had built up an idea of what it would be like and then to be confronted by the real thing. He wasn't quite as tall as I thought he'd be. His voice was a little different than what I had heard in his social media posts.

It was like the first time I had met someone really, truly famous. I was out with Dad, and we were out eating lunch at a deli in Beverly Hills. Burt Reynolds ended up in the booth next to us. He was old by that point, a little frail, but he was still Burt Reynolds. His image and the reality smashed together, and it was all a little disconcerting.

"You OK?" I asked Patrick, then immediately regretted it. Of course he wasn't. He'd been held hostage for over a week. Why was I even asking?

"I don't want to go back," he said quietly.

"I know." I nodded. "The police will be there. We'll call

your parents. They'll be happy to see you."

He looked at me. He didn't look happy.

My phone rang. Ito.

"Hey," I said.

"It's all clear. Go over there now. I'm in my car. I'll be there in ten minutes."

# 26

FIVE MINUTES LATER we were back on the formerly quiet street. Cop cars now lit it up, and all the neighbors were outside their front doors wondering what the hell had happened. This was a quiet valley neighborhood. This shit didn't happen *here*. Well, it never does until it does. Welcome to reality, friends.

A uniformed cop waved for me to stop my car. He leaned into my window to tell me that I couldn't go through, but I told him who I was and who was with me. He straightened up and waved me through.

I parked next to a police cruiser. I turned off the motor and said to Patrick, "Stay here."

He nodded.

I got out, wobbled a bit, and took a deep breath of night air. Cops were going in and out of the house. Some uniforms were talking with the neighbors, who shrugged and shook their heads; they hadn't see anything weird. Who sees anything weird?

There was an ambulance. Probably a little late for Edward.

"You look like shit," a voice said behind me.

I turned. Ito. Kemble was next to her.

"Where's Patrick?" she demanded.

I pointed to my car.

"Two bodies in three days," said Kemble, lumbering toward my car. "Must be a record."

Yay, me. I watched as Kemble waved for an EMT to join him. The detective opened the door, and the EMT started a quick exam of Patrick.

"You got blood on the back of your head," said Ito.

Right. The throbbing. "I got hit." I winced.

Ito sighed and nodded toward the ambulance. "They could check it out."

I shrugged.

"You're going to get it checked out, Jimmy," she ordered. Then she realized something. "Were you driving? In that condition?"

"I'm not going to lie to you. Let's just head over to the ambulance."

Her badass persona slipped a little, and I saw concern flash over her face. She walked me over and asked the remaining EMT to check out the back of my head. I sat off the back of the ambulance as he poked around. Which, of course, hurt. This begs the question: Why is it the first instinct of any medical professional to poke at a wound?

Ito watched Patrick, who was deep in conversation with Kemble. "How is he?"

"He's rattled. I don't blame him." I flinched at a particularly sharp poke and turned to the EMT. He didn't care and started cleaning the wound. I said to Ito, "He could use some sleep. In his own bed. Maybe you guys could talk to him tomorrow."

She turned to face me. "He's sort of a witness."

I shrugged. "I'm not saying he shouldn't talk, but look at him. He's just a kid."

"He's twenty." She put her hands on her hips. "Are you suggesting I let a material witness go home while there's at least one other suspect on the loose?"

"I'm a witness."

The EMT bandaged me up and told me I looked fine, but I might have a concussion. He asked if I had someone who could drive me home. I told him, yeah, sure. I sounded super convincing. Ito crossed her arms.

I gave in. "I'll call Erika," I said.

Satisfied, the EMT cleaned up the mess he had made patching me up and Ito went right back to the case. "And what exactly did *you* see?" she asked.

"Yes, Mr. Cooper, what *did* you see?" Agents Alexander and Martinez had shown up and were now standing so that they flanked me. No need to worry, agents: I'm no flight risk.

"Hey!" I said. "Everyone's here; this is great!"

Alexander folded her arms. Ito looked away, embarrassed.

"Well," I said, excited to have an audience, "I saw the guy that hit me." I paused. "Not *when* he hit me. After I woke up from being unconscious. Then I saw him." I made a face. "I'm a pretty terrible witness, aren't I?"

"Yeah, you are," answered Ito.

Another FBI agent approached Alexander. She leaned in, and as he spoke quietly, her face fell. "Shit," she said, then turned to Martinez. "The diamonds aren't here."

"The other guy has them," I offered. "Probably."

Alexander gave me the stink eye. "Why are you even here?"

"I am here *finding* Patrick Beverly." I pointed to him. "See, found him. I found him."

Alexander took a step closer and put up a finger. "I told you to let us handle it."

With both hands toward Patrick, I repeated, "But I found him! I found him!

"Jimmy..." cautioned Ito.

"Mr. Cooper, yes, indeed, you found him. I'm sure he's grateful." Alexander took a breath. "However, because of your rescue, there's fifty million dollars in diamonds somewhere in this city, there's at least one more man in the wind, and let's not forget about the dead body. So yeah. *Thanks*."

She nodded to Ito and then headed into the house, followed by Martinez.

Ito rolled her eyes back to me. "You had to go there, didn't you?"

I grunted. "I really thought I was..."

"The hero of this story?"

"Uh-huh." I blew air out through my lips. "For a hot second, I thought, yeah. I was the hero. But then she made some really good points."

"She did." Ito looked around. "Listen, I'd love to stay and chat, but I have work to do. I'm going to send someone over so you can give a statement."

"But you're right here. I'll tell you everything, Detective." I laid it on thick.

She wasn't buying. "Cute, but I think my boss might not agree with it. Given the nature of our relationship."

I stood up. "Our relationship. So we have a relationship?"

She considered the question and then turned and walked away.

"We don't have to do coffee next time," I shouted after her. "Maybe we're not get-coffee people. Maybe we're dinner people."

She turned and started walking backwards. "Or maybe we're not meant to be. "

Ito smiled, walking up the driveway, while I pondered just what the fuck she meant by that.

"You guys gross me out."

I looked to my left where Kemble was standing.

"Seriously, you guys. Gross."

He snorted and lumbered after his partner.

With the appreciation party over, I dug out my phone and called Erika. Lucky for me, it wasn't going to be the strangest call she had ever gotten from me. That would've been my call from inside It's a Small World After All in Disneyland while I was high and drunk out of my mind. I was supposed to do a live remote from there, promoting a Disney project that I was on.

Spoilers: They ended up going in a different direction.

I told her where I was and she said she'd be there in forty-five minutes. And that she loved me.

─ ──────── ─

FORTY MINUTES LATER, after giving a description of the vaping guy to an agent, I watched from the hood of my car as a black SUV came to a halt just at the police line. The backdoors popped open. Out jumped Eva Beverly and Robert Beverly. A uniformed officer made the mistake of trying to stop Eva, but he didn't realize he was in between her and her son. As she ran to Patrick, Robert quickly explained who they were.

Patrick had been talking to Agents Alexander and Martinez by the ambulance when he spotted his mother running toward him. He didn't move. His face didn't really change. Agent Alexander nudged him toward his mother and nodded that it was all right.

It didn't matter if he took a step or not. Eva was there and hugging him. Well. It wasn't a hug. It was an embrace. I couldn't blame her. I lost my favorite pair of shoes for a week, and I was beside myself the whole time. I wept like a baby when I found them under my bed. It's always the last place you look. Finding your kid is probably the same.

Eva looked like she was cradling a giant Ken doll as Robert approached. She reluctantly let go and Robert dutifully patted Patrick on his shoulder.

His actions were all so very... lukewarm. Rich people are so weird.

Robert turned himself away from his family reunion and strode over to me where I still sat on the hood of my car. "Thank you." He reached out, offering his hand, and I took it. Wow. A hand that shook thousands of deals into existence. "I won't forget what you've done for my family."

"As long as the check clears," I joked.

Robert's head tilted in confusion. After all, why wouldn't

his check clear?

"Sorry," I said, trying to salvage the now awkward situation. "I'm glad he's OK."

Robert nodded. He spotted his wife leading Patrick back to their car, continuing to faun over him. Robert followed.

A car horn sounded in the other direction. On the other side of the police line was my sister, standing outside her car, reaching back in through the window to honk the horn. The cops didn't want to let her pass.

# 27

___

WE WERE ON the 101 heading to my place. I grimaced as I gingerly poked at the wound at the back of my head. It must be human nature to jab at injuries. Apologies to that EMT.

"Edward Stratton is dead?" asked Erika, eyes on the road.

"Yeah. He caught me and Patrick escaping, I guess."

"And Patrick…"

I wiped my eyes, puzzling over what I should do about a possible concussion.

"He fought him off, it looks like," I said. "Probably saved my life."

Erika nodded, switched lanes, and asked, "So Edward killed Matty."

I shook my head — ow, ow, ow. "He wasn't there. He was

with the Beverlys. It must've been the other guy I followed. Or there's a third guy involved. Patrick didn't tell me. Patrick didn't tell me much in the car."

No one should expect him to be a Chatty Cathy.

"So that's it then," she said. I looked at her; and she glanced at me, and then put her eyes back on the road. "You found him. The job's done."

I shifted in my seat. "The guy that killed Matty is still out there. And the fifty million dollars."

"Yeah, but that's not your job."

It wasn't. True.

She said, "You got Patrick back. Can you let the FBI handle the rest?"

Gordon had always been good with boundaries. He drew them and expected people to honor them. That included work. He always made it clear to me, to my mother, and to the clients what was and wasn't his job. That was why he struggled being around me. Boundaries were not my thing.

"Jimmy?"

I give her a slight smile. "Just thinking." I was unsatisfied. Unsettled. I didn't like leaving it to the FBI to find Matty's killer. Not because they couldn't do it, but because I should have been a part of it. I owed Matty that.

And there was something else.

"It was weird watching Patrick when his parents came," I observed.

"What do you mean weird?"

I didn't know what I meant. I shook my head. "Just how they all acted."

"Rich people, Jimmy."

"Yeah, rich people."

There was something beyond that, though. I couldn't figure it out, and that bothered me.

After a quiet drive back home, save for a disagreement about which route to take, we rolled up to the bungalows in West Hollywood. The light was on in my place. Dad was up and waiting for me, I guess. I turned to Erika. "You want to come in? Say hi?"

She bit her bottom lip as she stared at my front window. She hadn't seen our dad in years, save for that hot second outside when I was trying to sneak him out of the building, and that had been almost two weeks ago. After she finished chewing on her lip, her face squished. She was debating the pros and cons.

"Just say hi," I said. "You don't have to stay long. It doesn't have to be a thing."

She shook her head. "Fuck it." Erika put her car into park and turned it off. She was out of the car before I could said anything else. She was knocking on the front door when I caught up to her.

"You don't have to knock," I said. "It's my place." I opened the door.

Dad was just getting up out of the couch as we stepped inside. "Hey, Jimmy..." He stopped talking when he saw Erika. "Hey. Peanut."

Fun fact: Erika hated that nickname. Even as a kid she would always say how demeaning it was.

"Hey, Dad."

The room became icy and tense as the two of them looked at each other, waiting for the other to speak.

"Water? Anyone?" I asked, hoping to break it up, make them act a little human.

Dad pointed toward the kitchenette. "There's pizza." He looked at me. "I didn't know when you'd be back, so I ordered."

"That's great, that's great." I pointed to Erika. "You want a slice?"

She shook her head.

Oh, yeah. This was going great.

"Well." I grinned. "I'm starving."

As I headed to the kitchen, I heard Dad take in a breath.

"What the fuck happened to you?" he demanded.

Erika answered, "He got knocked out."

"Knocked out?"

She nodded. "He's fine; he got it looked at."

Dad turned on me. "You got knocked out and you don't lead with that?"

I shrugged, opening the pizza box and snagging a slice of

pepperoni. "I didn't want it to be a thing."

My father was offended. "A thing? You didn't want it to be a thing? What the *hell* happened?"

"He rescued Patrick Beverly," said Erika. "Actually..." Lured by the smell, she met me in the kitchen and grabbed her own piece of pizza.

"It didn't go according to plan," I said.

"Jimmy, you can't be doing this," replied Dad. "They want to shoot the pilot at the end of this week."

"That's your concern?" snapped Erika. "He could've been killed."

Dad mustered a "Well, *yeah*." He looked back and forth between us, his face filled with worry. "I'm just saying..."

Erika dropped her unfinished pizza back into the box. "I'm out." She gave me a hug. "Don't die in the middle of the night."

"Wait — " I got out as she passed Dad on the way to the door.

"Peanut?" he mumbled, then checked with me. "What did I do?"

Her hand on the door, she gave him a look. I had seen that look a few times in my life. It meant that the person had stepped in it and really, *really* should know what they had done wrong. She shook her head. "Where to start? All the stuff in the past? Or maybe we can just do the present where you said 'Hey, let's get dinner' and then, *of course*, you didn't bother to follow up. But I'm *fine*. I'm worried what you're doing to Jimmy."

Dad's mouth opened and closed, looking for a rebuttal.

She didn't wait. "Night, Dad." And she was gone.

Dad looked at me, confused.

I put up my hand, following her out.

Erika had practically sprinted out the door, so she was back at her car and unlocking it before I caught up to her. "Erika?" She turned. "What happened in there, that was weird," I said. "You OK?"

"No. No, I am not." She pointed back to my place. "That man is dangerous."

"Uh, he's basically a marshmallow with arms and legs."

"Not *that* kind of dangerous, Jimmy," she said, exasperated. "He's *using* you."

"Of *course* he's using me. But... we're in a really good place."

Erika's eyes bugged out. "How can you — " She shook her head, she couldn't finish her thought. "Where do you think this is going?" She pointed at my bungalow. "You're in a good place. What does that mean?"

"It means we're healing; that's what it means."

She rolled her eyes now and shook her head. "*You* might be healing, but he's not. He sees you as a means to an end. He always has."

"He's different."

"You were almost killed tonight — "

" — I was not almost killed — "

" — and he only cared about how you're going to look on camera."

I bobbed my head. "Yes, *but*... he was concerned."

"Do you even hear yourself?"

My sister made a fair point. There was ample evidence in the story of my life that I couldn't hear the words coming out of my mouth. Certainly not until they were reflected back at me. Even then, it would take me a moment to register.

"Do you remember the first national commercial you booked?" she asked.

"The cereal commercial, yeah." I had made the mistake of eating the cereal over and over. No matter how good it is, you can't eat that much and not barf later.

"Do you remember auditioning for it?"

I didn't. Those kinds of things blur together after a while. One audition room starts to look like all the others, and you go to the same place over and over. I shook my head.

"*I* do. Because I was in the fifth grade, home sick, and you had the audition. Mom was working on a big case, and Dad" — she pointed to the house — "that man, was supposed to take care of me. I had a fever, a runny nose. What did he do?" She waited. "What do you think he did?"

I couldn't answer. I didn't remember. And I didn't want to guess.

"He pumped me full of Children's Tylenol, wrapped me in a blanket, and carried me along to *your* audition. I was there for almost two hours. He swore us both to secrecy so we wouldn't tell Mom."

I tried to think of something to say. Something that would comfort her. I couldn't come up with anything.

"He risked my health for a dumb audition, Jimmy."

"I did end up booking it."

That was a really dumb thing to say. I was totally missing her point.

"Fuck you, Jimmy." She got into her car.

"Erika, come on, I'm sorry. I shouldn't have said it."

She started her car and looked at me. "That man is always going to put *his* desires above anyone else's." She paused. "I'm glad you're not dead. Good night."

Throwing her car in reverse, she backed out and was gone. I watched as her car turned onto Sunset. I pushed out air and gave myself a failing grade on handling that situation. I headed back inside.

"Is she gone?" asked Dad.

"Yeah."

"She's mad at me?" he asked, though he knew the answer. He sheepishly rubbed his ear. "She always was a lot like your mother — always ready to go off on me." He shrugged. "I don't know what it is with those two."

I looked at him. "There's nothing wrong with those two.

You're just being an asshole, Dad."

# 28

ON TUESDAY MORNING, all the interested parties wanted to question Patrick again. The Beverlys had dictated the terms under which this would happen, and they told the FBI and the LAPD they would meet them at Cooper and Associates, with my mother representing Patrick. She was over the moon with excitement. This was the great, white whale. She was going to be the lawyer to a multibillionaire.

Much to my joyful surprise, I hadn't died from my head injury. I woke up with a massive headache and took some aspirin first thing, then resisted the urge to poke at the bandage. Now I was getting ready to head over to the office. While Dad was in the shower, I was in my kitchen, making coffee. It was then that I heard a cell phone ring.

Instinctively, I reached for my suit coat pocket. Then it rang again, and I realized it wasn't mine.

I walked over to the coffee table in front of the couch. Dad's phone was ringing — a call from Gail, the producer of the game show I had met a few days ago. I looked back toward the bathroom, where Dad was singing the Beach Boys' entire repertoire. He drifted from one set of lyrics to another, never landing on just one song. Infuriating.

Thinking it was important, I picked up and answered.

"Paul Cooper's phone, how may I direct your call?"

There was silence, and then Gail replied cautiously, "Jimmy?"

"Yep. Jimmy. Hey, Gail. How are you?" I winced. Sounding this chipper hurt, but I had a brand to maintain.

"I'm good."

She didn't sound good. Her breathing was shallow, and the words came out clipped. "So…" she began.

Producers don't just call to chitchat. They might start with chitchat, but the purpose of the call is *never* to catch up. They don't care. Producers need things. Time. Money. Catching up is not going to give them either of those.

"Yeah?"

"There's news," she spit out.

It was going to be bad news.

"It's not great."

Nailed it. I headed to the kitchen. Grabbing a mug, I tucked

Dad's phone into the crook of my shoulder and poured a cup of coffee. "The network is passing on the show?"

Another pause. "Well…"

I stopped. I knew what was coming. I had gotten a lot of calls like this. Normally they had come from my former agent, who would cough and hack her way through the call until she lit up another cigarette. So I supplied, "They're going in a different direction with casting?"

Relieved, Gail said, "Yeah." She took a breath. "We fought hard for you. But the network…"

Translation: Neither she nor Michael had fought hard for me, but she thought I needed to hear that. I didn't mind the lie. I took a sip of coffee, already feeling better.

Gail continued. "It's the stuff in the news, Jimmy. Everyone is talking about it. The murders, you know?"

I nodded, took another sip. "They do know I didn't kill anyone, right? Like, I'm not even a suspect. Arguably, I'm the hero."

She hummed. "I know. But, Jimmy, you're murder adjacent. You're right next to the murders. That's not the vibe the network is going for."

I took a breath. Honestly, I was feeling pretty good. "OK."

"I have to say, you're taking this well, Jimmy."

"Yeah, I am," I said, surprised at my own reaction. "It's almost like the game show didn't really mean anything to me. Huh."

This caused Gail to stumble over her words. "Oh! Uh. OK. That's... um... that's OK."

Ugh. Way to go, Jimmy. The show meant a lot to *her*.

"Well, you know, if things change..."

"Like if I become less 'murder adjacent'?" I offered.

"...maybe you can be on the show."

I laughed quietly. "Take care, Gail." I hung up.

"That my phone?"

Dad was dressed in a golf shirt and still drying his hair. I handed him the phone, saying, "Gail called."

"Shit, shit! This was about the shooting schedule." He started unlocking his phone, ready to call back.

"Don't worry about it," I said. "They're going in a different direction."

He looked at me, growing pale. "A different direction?" He licked his lips.

I nodded. "It's all the stuff in the news about me and the case. The network... You know how scared networks are of..." I paused. "Right, well, they don't like cast members being associated with death and crime and stuff. So..."

Dad looked at his phone. I could see the wheels turning in his head. "I could call her back," he muttered. "I should call her back."

"It's out of her hands, Dad. And she sounded relieved. It's over."

He looked at me, though his eyes seemed a little distant.

He never did like losing a role.

"We'll get them next time," I said.

He nodded. "Yeah. That's the spirit," he said quietly. "Next time."

My phone dinged — a text from Patrick's friend Blake.

*Duuuude. That guy that took Patrick, he was the old guy at the party.*

I texted a thanks back. About a day late, Blake.

———

THE VIBE IN the law offices of Cooper and Associates was "Cautiously Excited." Everybody from reception to the other attorneys knew who was coming. There had never been such a thrilling cast of characters in the office at one time. Not just the Beverlys, but the LAPD! The F-B-Freakin'-I! Can I get a "Federal Jurisdiction in the house!" Wut-wut!

None of this was normal. Until today, I had been the biggest celebrity to walk through the door.

Nora met me at reception, offering me a glass of water. "Coffee is a bad idea. Better to stay hydrated with a concussion."

Of course my morning coffee had been a bad idea. Taking the glass, I said, "How did you hear?"

"Your sister told me." She and I started walking. "Ms. Cooper is waiting for you in your office."

"Are they here yet?"

"The Beverlys?" Nora shook her head. "They should be in at any moment. The FBI and the LAPD are in the conference room. Your mother is in her office. She's been on the phone with the Beverlys."

We arrived at my office, and I stepped inside as Nora headed to her desk. Erika was sitting on my black leather couch, reading through a folder of documents. Her eyes flicked up to me and back down to the pages. "How are you feeling?" she asked, distantly.

She was still upset about last night, but being my kid sister, couldn't help but check in.

I sat next to her. "About what I said last night…"

"You were dumb?" she offered without looking away from the file.

"I wouldn't be me if I didn't say dumb and inappropriate things from time to time."

She looked up and raised an eyebrow. "That's true." She blinked and shook her head. "I don't know what the story is between you and Dad right now. Maybe he has turned a corner. Maybe he's not the guy he was. But I'm not ready to believe that."

I nodded. She nodded. My face squished from the throbbing pain the nodding had kicked off. Erika stopped nodding. "Are you OK?"

I showed her the glass of water. "I'm staying hydrated."

She smiled.

"What are you reading?" I asked.

"Evidence." She closed the folder. "The Beverlys gave Mom evidence that Edward Stratton had been stealing money from them. They're going to turn it over to the FBI and the police."

"Really?" I took the folder from her and opened it. The bank accounts and transactions inside it made my head swim. "This is real? This all makes sense to you?"

Erika took the folder back. "It does. And it is. Up until about two months ago, he had been funneling money out of the company." She tapped the folder. "Bits and pieces here and there. It all adds up to a lot of money."

"He stopped two months ago?"

She shrugged. "Maybe he wanted a bigger piece and came up with the kidnapping idea."

I leaned back and twirled the glass in my hands. "Yeah, maybe. Are the Beverlys saying why Edward needed the money?"

"Mom didn't tell me if they did. She's keeping the Beverlys to herself."

I nodded and finished off the water. Our mother could be a bit of a control freak. "They sure got the evidence fast."

"What do you mean?"

"Doesn't this kind of accounting" — I pointed to the folder — "you know, where the accountants dig through all the stuff and find the secrets…?"

She sighed. "You mean forensic accounting?"

"Yes, *that*. I do mean that. That stuff takes time."

"It can." Erika thought about it. "Once they were onto Edward, they started looking. Edward was head of security, not an accountant. Maybe he was terrible at covering his tracks."

"Maybe." I chewed my lip.

A knock at the door and Nora leaned in. "They're here."

Erika and I stepped out of my office into the hallway to watch, along with everyone else, as Mom escorted the Beverlys through Cooper and Associates. She was chatting to Robert Beverly on her right. He was dressed in his suit of choice: dark blue, double-breasted, with gold buttons. He nodded brusquely as Mom spoke. Behind them were Eva and Patrick. She was dressed in a cream-colored suit while Patrick was in a shirt and tie, which made him look twelve years old.

I guess there had been a discussion about dressing up for your police interview.

As they got closer, I joined the group. Mom and Robert glanced at me but then carried on with their whispered conversation.

"How are you, buddy?" I said to Patrick. We were almost to my mother's office. Once inside, she wouldn't want me there. They had stuff to go over, and I'd mess it all up. "I just wanted to ask you about Friday night."

Eva stopped and turned to me. Everyone else followed suit. Mom looked at me, raising an eyebrow. Robert looked at his wife and then to his son. Patrick stood behind his mother, staring at me with sullen eyes.

"He's not going to do that. All right?" she snapped. "He is here to speak to the police. And you are not the police."

I was taken aback by her hostility toward me. I had thought we were on the same page. This wasn't how I'd expect someone to act after I just saved their son.

She started to go, but I stepped toward her and Eva stopped again.

"I just want to know if he recognized the guy who stabbed Matty. Was it the guy I followed, or was it — "

"James," said my mother sharply.

I looked at the group. "I'm just trying to find out who killed Matty."

"And the police will do their best once they have spoken with Patrick," replied my mother. "Now, Mr. and Mrs. Beverly, Patrick, right this way."

The group moved farther down the hall, and Patrick gave me a cursory once-over before dismissing me entirely. I didn't want to tell anyone, but at that moment, I was staring to not like this Beverly kid. I didn't want to shit on a kidnap victim, but this kid was an asshole, not at all the person I thought he was.

# 29

"JUST LET THEM take it from here," suggested Gordon. I had called him after spending ten minutes outside my mother's office, hoping that I would hear something of Patrick's statement through the closed door that would get me closer to the guy that stabbed Matty.

Spoilers: I did not.

Agents Alexander and Martinez had given me a cold reception as they walked into my mother's office. That was followed by an equally cold one from Ito as she passed me. Detective Kemble, on the other hand, chuckled, slapping me on the shoulder. He kept it up until the door closed in my face.

Not quite the reception I had expected for finding Patrick

Beverly. Some of it I could chalk up to professional jealousy; after all, it seemed, I was the one closing the case. But the Beverlys? Especially how Eva treated me? I just didn't get it.

After Nora caught me with my ear pressed against the door, I reconsidered my choices and called Gordon Bixby.

"I don't know, Gordon. If I had let them take it, Patrick could still be a hostage — or worse."

"Jimmy," he said flatly, "I don't know if this is quite the win you think it is."

I put my feet up on my desk and looked out at the view. It was another clear morning, and I could see all the way to the ocean, where the moisture hadn't burnt off yet. "Patrick is back home; the guy behind the whole thing is dead. Those diamonds are hot as fuck, so what are the chances the guys involved are going to be able to fence them? This is the easy part."

Gordon cleared his throat. I could hear him shift in his chair. "Let's reconsider being involved. You haven't made friends with the FBI, and it doesn't sound like your girl Ito is particularly happy with you."

"She's not my girl. And like, 'my girl'? Who says that anymore? Are we going to do the Twist at the sock hop later?"

He snorted. "My point is — "

"I understand your point." I sighed. I didn't want to tell him how much I hated the situation. It didn't seem right to walk away now. I turned away from the view. "How can I let them handle finding Matty's killer?"

"I know how you're feeling, being so close to the finish line, but you gotta let them take it the rest of the way."

It was sound advice coming from a man who really knew what he was talking about.

Gordon sighed. "But you're not going to do what I'm suggesting, are you?"

"I'd love to Gordon..."

He grunted, then said, "You get in their way, they'll arrest you for interfering."

"The LAPD wouldn't do that again."

"I'm talking about the FBI. Don't fuck around with them, James."

I nodded. "I promise. I won't fuck around with them."

Another voice asked, "Won't fuck around with who?" It was my mother, standing in my doorway.

I covered the phone with my hand. "Mom, don't you knock?"

"Is that Greta?" asked Gordon.

"I don't have to knock. I own the place," she answered.

"Yes, it is," I said into the phone. Then I asked my mom, "What are you doing here?"

"They're on a break."

"How's she doing?" asked Gordon.

I was beginning to get a headache.

"Who are you talking to?" Mom asked as she examined

one of the chairs in front of my desk. She didn't look pleased. I don't know why. She was the one who choose all of the furniture.

"It's Gordon."

Her face brightened as she sat down. "And how is he?"

I couldn't do it anymore. "Gordon, I'll call you back." I hung up, not waiting for him to say goodbye.

"James!" exclaimed Mom. "You could have let me say hello. Find out how he is."

"He's great. You should call him." I put my phone on the desk. "What is happening in there?"

She huffed, annoyed at me. "I don't have time to call Gordon."

I shook my head. "I'm not a messenger service."

"Tell him, next time — "

"What. Is. Happening. In there?"

"You couldn't tell from your eavesdropping?"

I chewed my lip.

She gave me a rueful smile. "I suspected as such." She shook her head. "Please don't do that. That's incredibly unprofessional. Unethical." She paused. "And embarrassing."

"Fine. I won't do it. Now, can you tell me what's going on in there?"

Mother crossed her arms. "Patrick is a very good witness. Detailed. The agents seemed very pleased."

"You don't." I pointed out.

She didn't answer.

"Has he said who stabbed Matty?"

My mother shook her head. "We haven't gotten there yet."

"What about the other men, besides Edward? Has he talked about them?"

"James," she began, "I'm not sure I should tell you."

I frowned.

"You want to remain involved in the case."

I didn't answer.

She tipped her head. "I don't see why I should *help* you remain involved. Everything is fine now."

"Is it?"

"James…"

I leaned forward. "I just can't sit around and do nothing."

"There's plenty of work to be done." She pointed to the door. "I'm sure Nora has some cases for you."

"I'm sure she does. But I'm not done with this one."

There was a gentle knock at the door. Erika was there. "They're ready for you again."

Mom pushed herself off her chair. "James, find something new." She headed out of the office, walking past Erika.

"Great talk, Mom!" I called after her.

Erika observed me from the door.

"Do *you* want to tell me what's going on in there?" I asked.

"What, give you a little inside information?" she said,

walking into the room and closing the door behind her.

"You have any?"

She shook her head. "Mom is handling it."

I sucked my lip, disappointed.

"I want to figure this thing out." I looked at the ceiling. "Edward Stratton, head of security to actual billionaires, needs money. First, he tries to steal it. Then, he decides that's not enough, and now he's going to kidnap and hold their heir for ransom." I shook my head, not understanding.

"The FBI is at his home, going over everything. I'm sure a motive will come out," she said, sitting in the very same chair Mom had just vacated.

I looked around the room and started spitballing. "Maybe he had a gambling problem. He liked drugs. Women."

"Fast cars?" suggested Erika.

"Cute." I put my elbows on my desk and cradled my face. "This is important. And what's the connection between him and the other guys?" I thought about it some more. "He wouldn't use his own guys. Would he? They might be loyal to the job and not him."

Erika shrugged. "Money has a way of changing people's loyalty."

I dismissed it. "The guy I followed — the one with the Lakers jersey — he didn't strike me as professional security." I chewed at my lip now. There was something I was forgetting. Then I remembered. "Two months ago."

"Two months ago?"

"Eva Beverly told me that Edward changed about two months ago."

Erika nodded. "What happened two months ago?"

I looked at her. "I don't know."

"You don't know?" She paused. "Aren't you the detective?"

I smirked. "How long do you think they're going to be in there for?"

Erika looked in the direction of our mother's office. "Hours, probably. Why?"

I shrugged. "I thought I'd spend some time being a detective while the grown-ups are busy."

# 30

I GAVE A cursory wave to Derrick Sayles's receptionist as I strode past her desk, heading into the inner sanctum. She gripped her phone as she stood up. "You can't go back there without an appointment!" she shouted in her terse Long Island growl.

I gave a wave back. "I'm just looking for the bathroom."

She huffed and turned to her desk. Guess she didn't believe me.

Derrick's phone had just started chirping when I found his office. It was wide with a view of Wilshire Boulevard. He was heading back to his desk, lawbook in hand, wearing a gray suit with a loosened red tie. Sensing me at his door, he looked at me, a little confused.

I pointed at the phone on his desk as I walked in. "That's your receptionist. There's someone running around your office without an appointment."

He took a settling breath, put the book down, and picked up the phone. I sat down in the leather chair in front of his desk, the one reserved for clients. I couldn't hear exactly what his receptionist said, but the message was clear. She was angry I had upset the way things were done around here.

"It's all right, Maggie. It's fine."

She said something else.

Derrick glanced at me before answering. "No. You don't need to call Ricky."

That was a relief, actually. I wasn't all that excited to see Ricky. I had things to do today, and getting my ass handed to me would only slow me down.

Derrick hung up and sat down.

"Nice office," I said. "It fits you." The windows were large, the furniture pricey and ostentatious; perfect for a man with big ambitions. Derrick had decorated to impress...or was it more aspirational?

He kept looking at me.

"Is this where you threaten me with a restraining order?" I asked. "Because last time you saw me, you said — "

Derrick put up a hand. "Last time, I lost my temper." He gave a slight shrug. "I didn't fully understand the situation and lost my temper."

Interesting.

He leaned back and steepled his fingers. "What can I do for you, Mr. Cooper?"

"I want to talk about two months ago." I crossed my legs and settled into the chair. It was quite comfortable. I was starting to see where Mom was coming from with my own office chairs.

"Two months ago? Why?"

"That is the question, right?"

He shook his head. I had him turned around. "Why are you here? Patrick was found," he said. "And it was the head of security. Inside job." He shook his head and pointed at himself. "Told you I had nothing to do with it."

"Yeah, well, sorry about that."

He laced his fingers together. "Lawyers, we get a bad rap."

I nodded.

"I want to talk about that head of security. You ever see him around Patrick?"

Derrick's eyes narrowed. "What are you getting at?"

"I'm just trying to find out if he's connected to Patrick's business. Maybe he got involved." I scratched at the back of my head. "Maybe he lost money like you. Could be he took it personal like you. Holding Patrick for ransom would solve two birds with one stone."

Was I mixing metaphors?

Derrick gazed at me for a moment. Finally, he said,

"What's the game here?"

I cocked my head but didn't answer.

He sat up and pulled his chair closer to his desk. He started fiddling with a pen in his left hand. "Are you still working with the Beverlys?"

"Sure," I lied. They were still over in Century City, and technically I hadn't been told I *wasn't* working for them. Derrick didn't need to know that.

"Do you want me to say that Edward was…" He searched for the word. "Involved?"

What was he talking about? Why was he asking me what *I* wanted? It suddenly I felt like someone overhauled the script of this scene and I hadn't been told. I decided to press ahead anyway. "Was he?"

Derrick eyed me. "He could've been."

I shook my head and gave a half smile. Derrick was dancing around something and wasn't just going to come out and say it. What had I stumbled into? I was afraid to ask him directly. He might shut up.

Derrick peeked toward the door. Then he tapped his fingers and said quietly, "Is this a test?"

Well, well. Maybe it was. "You tell me."

His demeanor changed then, his cockiness dissolving. "Everyone is cool. More than cool." He spoke like he was sharing a secret, one he was happy to be on the inside of. "Like I said, I'm good. I'm whole. That's all that I ever wanted." He offered me an easygoing smile. "No hard feelings. Water under the bridge."

"Riiiight," I said, drawing the word out. "*Everyone* is cool?" I wondered who everyone was and what made them cool.

Derrick nodded quickly. "That's my impression. I haven't talked to everyone personally. Some of them are, quite frankly, best left alone..." He frowned. "That was the whole point in paying everyone off, right? To make this go away."

I nodded.

He leaned back again, like there wasn't a problem in the world. "So, anything I can do... as long as it's not too illegal." He chuckled.

I smiled and played along. It seemed like Patrick's debts to everyone he had made bad deals with had been paid. Did he do it? Or his parents?

"So we're good?" Derrick concluded.

Time to roll the dice.

"Patrick will be happy to know that everyone is cool."

"Patrick? What does he have..." Derrick's face went pale as he realized I wasn't *also* on the inside. "Oh, shit."

So Robert, not Patrick, had paid off the debt. What was going on?

Derrick shook his head, looking disappointed. He reached for his phone and jabbed a button. "Ricky?"

I didn't wait around to see what sort of mood Ricky was in. I got up and out of the chair and was down the hall before

I heard what Derrick had to say next, and I was at Maggie's desk in the lobby when I started hearing heavy feet behind me. Maggie gave me the stink eye. I paused and announced to the waiting clients, "Best meeting ever. Five stars. Y'all are in for a real treat."

I went through the brown doors and didn't wait for the elevator. The stairs were the quickest way out.

Back on Wilshire, catching my breath, wiping sweat from my face, trying to shake off the dull thumping in the back of my head, I realized I still hadn't gotten what I needed. What had happened two months ago?

I texted Liza Borden, the ex-girlfriend. She had said she had dated Patrick for about three months, which fell into my mystery period of time. Maybe she could answer my questions.

She texted back, saying she was over near Culver City at a space on Exposition Boulevard. She explained she was rehearsing with her band before going out on tour. She wondered if it could wait and I said it couldn't. The man responsible for Matty's death was out there. She told me to come over so we could talk.

Twenty minutes later, I walked in on the four-piece band in the middle of a rumbling rocker. Liza stood at a microphone, holding a guitar papered over with stickers. She wore a vintage AC/DC T-shirt from the Back in Black Tour and ripped jeans. She spotted me, nodded, but kept going through the song until it ended with a flourish. Liza gave a couple of notes to the bass player, who nodded and plucked as he listened, and then turned to me.

"Let's do a quick five," she said and pulled off her guitar, sticking it on a stand.

I watched the band disperse.

"So you found him," Liza said to me as she walked over. "Congratulations."

"Yeah." I ruffled the hair at the back of my head. "It didn't go exactly how I wanted it."

"Yeah," she said empathetically. "Matty Goodman. I used to watch him too."

"He had a lot of fans," I replied.

She agreed and pointed to the bandage on the back of my head. "You OK?"

"It hurts when I poke at it."

Liza frowned, "Why would you poke it?"

"To see if it hurts?" I shrugged. "I want to ask you more about your time with Patrick. About two months ago?"

"Sure." Liza grabbed a metal water bottle from a nearby stool. "What do you need to know?"

"That's the thing, I don't know." I pulled out my phone and brought up a picture of Edward Stratton. "Did you ever see this guy hanging around?"

She took my phone, sniffed a little, and cleared her throat. "Yeah. I saw him around. Not at the beginning, but yeah, suddenly he was there a lot. About two months ago, now that you mention it."

I took my phone back. "Did Patrick explain why?"

Liza thought about it, then shook her head. "Not really. But, like, that was pretty common with Patrick. Everything was 'great' even when it wasn't, you know? It's that business world bullshit..." She wiggled her fingers in the air like she was casting a spell. "That everything was always great. He and that guy" — she pointed at my phone — "they would huddle and talk. Really intense."

"He never said anything?"

"Nah. Listen, it was already the beginning of the end for me and Patrick. The people he was meeting with, the ones that I saw, it changed. They got creepier. That lawyer guy that tried to fuck up Patrick? He started showing up." She sighed. "It was intense sometimes. Patrick snapped at me more often, which, like, *nooooo.*"

I nodded. It sounded like this was around the time Patrick blew the deal with Derrick Sayles and a bunch of other "investors."

"Did you ever see a guy with Edward? A white guy, taller than me, blond, in pretty good shape, maybe a Lakers fan?"

"With Edward, no. But..." she thought a moment. "That sounds a lot like Benny."

"Benny?"

She groaned. "Benjamin Lesser was his name. He wanted

us to call him Bad Benny."

"*Bad* Benny?"

"Yeah. It's dumb, isn't it?" she said before taking another drink of water. "He was trying to burnish a reputation. Thought of himself as a tough guy."

I nodded. "You said he wasn't with Edward."

"Yeah." She closed her water bottle. The band was trickling back in. "He was a friend of Patrick's."

"What?"

She put up a hand, pausing to clarify. "He was a friend of a friend, I mean. Like, it was a social scene, man."

"Benjamin Lesser."

"That's probably the guy." The band was picking up their instruments. "Look, I gotta get back. I'm renting this place by the hour." She did a half-hearted wave goodbye and returned to her rehearsal. She named a song and the drummer counted them in. The band erupted into a hooky tune.

As I headed outside, I checked my phone. It had been a few hours. I might be running out of time.

Sitting in my car, it took me twenty minutes, but I finally found an address. It wasn't far. Benjamin Lesser lived in an apartment off of West Olympic just next to Beverly Hills. When I got there fifteen minutes later, I suspected I might be onto something.

Bad Benny's apartment had three cop cars in front of it.

# 31

—

SO THE COPS had gotten here first. What were the chances it was just a coincidence? About zero, I decided as I parked, especially since I had spotted Agents Alexander and Martinez stepping out of a black SUV.

The apartment was a stone and stucco building from the mid-sixties, three stories with parking all around the ground floor. It probably had a pool in a central courtyard that only got sun an hour a day, when it was directly overhead.

With the cops getting to him first, it was going to be that much harder to question Bad Benny and find his partner.

I was about to step out of the car when the possibility of taking to Benny got even more complicated. "Oh, shit," I mumbled.

Coming down the center of the street was the coroner's van. Two guys hopped out of the front and headed to the back doors. A minute later, they pushed a stretcher and an empty body bag across the street toward the building.

My curiosity got the best of me, so I jumped out of the car and headed to the front door of the apartment complex just as the guys from the coroner's office arrived.

"Let me help you with that," I said, holding the door for them as they rolled the gurney in. The guy at one end nodded his thanks.

His colleague was jabbing at the elevator button as I followed them into the complex. Yep, there was a pool in the middle, with apartments ringing around the two floors above me. Residents had stepped out of their front doors and were all staring in the same general direction — up and across. I stepped farther in and took a look.

Up on the third floor, on the street side, an apartment had been taped off. A group of cops and FBI agents stood outside. I saw Agent Martinez chatting with a woman I assumed was a resident.

I headed up the stairs.

I was a little winded, but I got up there in time to watch the cops part ways to let the stretcher into the apartment. I followed, leaving confused looks in my wake. I had learned a long time ago: walk like you belong. It was the only way to survive the red carpets alongside *real* movie stars.

Bad Benny was dead. His body was laying in the middle of his small living room made even smaller by the number of authority figures standing around him. The coroner herself had finished, and her two staffers were just about to lift the body onto the stretcher. Benny was on his back, his eyes half closed. The red halo around his head meant the back of his head was probably caved in. He was in shorts and a Lakers T-shirt. This guy was a fan until the very end.

The place looked like it had been turned over. There was a couch against the wall; a couple of recliners faced a TV to my right. On my left was the kitchen and dining area with a hallway probably leading to the bathroom and one or two bedrooms.

"Jesus Christ," a voice grumbled. Kemble was by the kitchen, small notebook in hand. "Are you, like, cursed or something?"

"Only when I see you, Kemble."

He gave me the finger.

"What are you doing here, Mr. Cooper?" Agent Alexander walked in from the hallway, Ito was behind her.

"I followed a lead."

She didn't take the bait. "Well, this is an active crime scene so I'm going to have to ask you to leave."

"But I just got here."

Agent Alexander crossed her arms. Clearly, she wasn't one for banter. Ito looked down at the floor and shook her head.

"So," I continued. "Bad Benny is dead."

"Bad Benny?" asked Alexander, raising an eyebrow.

"Just a nickname he tried to make happen." I looked around the room, trying to take it all in. "Did you know he was friends with Patrick?"

"Friends?" said Ito.

I clarified, "I was told 'friend of a friend.' But he knew him." The look on their faces — from Ito's knit brow to Kemble's one-step-behind stare — told me they hadn't known that. "How did you guys find him?"

Ito offered it up. "Turns out the Jetta in the driveway at the house..."

I remembered that Jetta. My knee still ached.

"It was a rental." She nodded toward the body. "He used his own name."

"What an idiot," offered Kemble.

Alexander cleared her throat. Kemble looked properly chastised.

I looked around. "So what are we thinking? Conspirators not getting along?"

"Mr. Cooper, this is an active, ongoing — "

"You said that. I heard that. We don't need to do that over."

Alexander closed her eyes and took a breath. "You're not going to go away, are you?"

"I'm already *here*," I said. "So, what happened?"

Alexander didn't reply, but Ito cut the tension. "Units reported to a call about a loud fight. When they arrived, the door was opened and..." She pointed to the body. "Took some time to connect the victim to one of our suspects."

"What did they fight about?" I asked.

No one answered.

"No one heard what the fight was about?"

Ito said, "The neighbors next door didn't hear anything. They have kids and were distracted."

"We're still questioning everyone in the building, OK?" said Alexander. "That fine with you?"

As I shrugged, there was a sudden commotion behind me.

"Detectives!" shouted one of the crime scene specialists. I turned and saw him lifting a very familiar briefcase from behind the couch.

Alexander strode past me and slipped on some latex gloves. She dialed the combination lock — she must've gotten it from the Beverlys — and popped it open.

And there they were. The diamonds. Still there. Still shiny as ever.

She closed the case, literally and figuratively. "All right. Let's see if we can lift some fingerprints. Maybe we'll get lucky." As she followed one of her underlings out of the apartment, Alexander looked quite pleased.

I made a face. Something wasn't right. "That was pretty

easy," I said. Everyone looked at me. "It was behind the couch. Don't you think that was a little convenient? Like, wow, what a *fantastic* hiding place."

Kemble frowned. "It was hidden, Cooper."

"Yeah?"

"It was out of *sight*," he said, doubling down.

"Would you put fifty million dollars' worth of diamonds behind a couch?"

He folded his arms. "We aren't dealing with geniuses here." Then he turned back to his work.

"Yeah," I said quietly. But there was just something *off*.

And then it clicked. It was something big.

I turned to Ito. I had to talk to her. I had to explain it to her because if my theory was dumb, I'd rather she was the only one to hear it. I stepped closer to her. "I need to tell you something."

"Yeah, me too," she replied. She looked around the room. "But let's take it outside."

We stepped outside of the apartment and walked about twenty feet away near another apartment.

Ito started, "OK, listen — "

"Can I go first?"

"First?"

I nodded.

She glanced back at the apartment then back at me. "I really need to get this off my chest."

"OK, but I really think you'll want to hear this."

She put a hand up. I shut up.

"I want to say I'm sorry," she began. "I've been weird around you the past few days."

That's not what I had expected her to say, but happy to take it. "Apology accepted. Now — "

"I'm not done."

"There's more?" I wondered.

"Yes. More," she said, peeved. "You want to hear it?"

It sounded like I really should. I nodded.

"If we're going to do this," she continued, "we have to have some ground rules."

"Ground rules. That sounds great. Now — "

"Jimmy! Let me *finish*." Violet took a breath and looked at me. I sometimes forgot how beautiful her eyes were. "Given our jobs, it's not always going to be easy to have face to face moments." She looked back at the crime scene. "And I hate that we keep meeting over dead bodies, but here we are." She turned back to me. "I'm trying to take advantage of the present moment to tell you something."

I rubbed my head. "Yes. Right. Finish."

It took her a moment to collect herself. Finally, she said, "It's hard for cops to date civilians."

I nodded. "I get that. I was an actor. When you're an actor, you can only date actors. Normies just don't get it."

She paused, trying to decide if I was serious.

I was.

"Jimmy," she went on, "as a cop, there's going to be shit that I can't tell you. That you can't know. And I realized, there's going to be times that you won't want to tell me things. You'll want to play things close to the vest."

"Those are called secrets."

"Shut *up*. I was really pissed about you not telling me about Patrick Beverly's kidnapping. But." She pointed between me and her. "We're going to have to be cool with each other holding things back."

I wanted to make sure I got what she was saying. "You want me to be cool with us keeping secrets from each other."

"Yes." She corrected herself. "I mean *professional* secrets. That's the ground rule."

"OK."

"Really?" she said, raising both eyebrows.

I froze, realizing that I was missing what she was really saying. "So. Wait. So you *are* into me?"

She frowned and pulled her head back. "Into you?"

I waved my hands, trying to save this moment. "I don't mean that in a creepy way. You've been talking in a very emotionally honest way, and I'm just not used to that. This is my way of saying, we're going to try this. Whatever this is."

Ito's face relaxed with a little bit of a smile. "Yes. We're going to try this."

I took a breath, enjoying the possibilities.

She reclined against the apartment wall. She looked relieved to get that off her chest. "Now, what do you want to tell me?"

Oh. Right. I was a detective on a case.

"I don't think there was another kidnapper."

# 32

---

"WOULD YOU SLOW down?" asked Ito. I was weaving through traffic, heading west on the 10. "Cannonball" by the Breeders was on, and I was in a mood.

"I'll start over," I said without taking my eyes off the road.

"I meant the *car*," she stated, her eyes also glued to the freeway. "We're not in pursuit of anyone."

It took me a minute, but yeah, she was right. We weren't in actual pursuit of anyone. I was just impatient. I took us down from ninety miles an hour to the normal seventy-five for the 10. "Where was I?"

I had been going through my theory since we got into my car. She had no longer been needed at the crime scene. It belonged to the feds' anyway. And Kemble was happy to see me go.

"Two months ago," she answered, her eyes still on the road.

"Right. *Right.* Something happened two months ago. You know what happened two months ago?"

"I'm assuming you're going to tell me, Jimmy." She pointed at a car that I was gaining on too fast.

I switched lanes and said, "Edward stopped taking money."

"I know that. I saw the evidence."

I nodded. "Yes, but why? Why did he stop taking the money? I think it's because *maybe* he got caught."

She frowned, but I didn't answer the unasked question.

"You know who also needed money? You don't have to guess. I'll tell you." I changed lanes again, moving farther to the left. "Patrick. Patrick Beverly also needed money. Lots of it. And I think he went looking for it in the same way Edward did."

"Patrick tried to funnel money out of his parents' finances?"

I nodded, trying to suppress a smile at my cleverness. Nobody likes a gloating clever person. "Appearances aside, he's not a dumb rich kid. He made some bad deals and owed people money. He couldn't go to his parents because they would find out what he was doing. So he went into their accounts. He goes in and he spotted a problem." I braked hard to avoid tapping the bumper of a Honda Civic.

"I told to you to *slow* down."

I waved in agreement but kept going, excited. "The problem is, if he could find Edward's siphoning of funds, some accountant just might do the same thing. Because Edward did it first, he, in fact, *spoiled* Patrick's plan."

Ito raised an eyebrow, turning to me. "Patrick kidnapped himself?"

I paused. "What a way to step on my line, but *yes*. Patrick came up with this idea." I nodded as I kept talking. "It's sort of diabolical. He'd get the money he needed, but, of course, he couldn't do it alone. He got Edward to help."

"How?"

"The evidence that you got? It was also leverage." I shrugged. "Edward didn't want to do this. The moment I met him, he didn't like me. He resented me. And yet he wasn't lying when he told me that he was the one who had recommended me to the Beverlys. And Matty."

"Because it was Patrick's idea."

I made a face. I didn't like this next bit. "Agent Alexander was right, but not about who. We were hired because we were idiots."

Ito shook her head. "You're not an idiot."

I took my eyes off the road to nod a thanks to her. "In order for their plan to work though, they needed one other person."

"Bad Benny?"

"They needed someone else to be the bagman at the parking lot for the exchange. This way Edward would have an alibi because he would be with the Beverlys."

"How can you be so sure that Benny was the only other kidnapper? Patrick gave a description."

"Sure, sure," I said sarcastically. "Patrick couldn't *possibly* have made that up?"

"Jimmy," she warned.

"What? He's the only person alive who can describe the other guy. Because I can't. I was hit from behind. Disorientated. And the diamonds? Hidden behind the couch? If there was someone else, an actual third man, he killed Benny over the diamonds and then just left?"

"He ran out of time. Someone heard the argument."

I shook my head. "No one heard the argument. I bet whoever called it in wasn't a neighbor."

Ito said nothing.

"The crime scene was a setup." I stole a glance at her. "The call to the cops. The diamonds behind the couch. We were meant to find them. Benny was a loose end. The diamonds were a loose end. Now all of them are tied up."

"Patrick?"

I nodded. "It all blew up in his face. When Matty decided to tackle Bad Benny — "

"Are we really calling him that?" she muttered, but I

continued.

"When Matty knocked down Bad Benny, Patrick saw it all going wrong and he couldn't let that happen. He owed money to dangerous people. So he got out of the car, took me out, and stabbed Matty."

Ito stared at the traffic ahead of us for a long time.

I went over the highlights again. "Patrick desperately needed money. He didn't go to his parents because he didn't want to look like a failure. His ex-girlfriend told me he was armed and paranoid." I paused. "OK, she didn't say he was paranoid and didn't say he carried a knife..."

Finally, she said, "Do you have any evidence?" She looked at me. "This all sounds circumstantial..." She shook head, turning her attention back to the highway.

She was right, of course. I didn't have any evidence. But I knew I was right. I could feel it in my bones. Everything just fit together. I exited the 10 and got on the 1, heading north toward the Palisades. I put on a grin. "OK, you got me. I'm a little light on evidence. But..."

"Jesus, Jimmy," she said under her breath.

"No, no. I *got* this. Patrick's going to confess. Or he'll slip up. And boom! We got him. You slap on the cuffs, and we go out for dinner. My treat." I looked at her, but she didn't meet my eyes.

Fifteen minutes later, we pulled up to the gate of the Beverlys' home. The FBI were gone, but there was a feeling of the house was still under siege. The guard in the little shack didn't even bother to get off his stool. With a small, suspicious shake of his head, he seemed to remember me from the weekend when the FBI had to stop his boss from strangling me.

I tried a smile and hooked a thumb over at Ito. "She's a cop," I said, as if that was the password.

"Oh, yeah?" he said. He put his phone aside and stood, then pulled at his belt and leaned down, peering deeper into my car.

I looked over at Ito, who was staring ahead, seemingly over this whole encounter.

"Hey," I said. She turned to me. "Come on." I nodded encouragingly. "Do your thing."

She took a deep, annoyed breath and pulled her badge off her waistband to show the guard.

He chewed his cheek. "I'll have to call."

"Yep," she replied.

"Wait here," he told us as he stepped back into his shack.

"As if we were going someplace else, right?" I snorted.

Ito said nothing.

The guard was on the phone for longer than anyone needed to be to announce a visitor. As I watched him talk, I drummed my fingers on the steering wheel. "What is taking them so long?" I was ready to get this show going.

That question seemed to pique Ito's interest. "Well,"

she mused, "if you'd done something wrong, wouldn't you hesitate to invite a police officer into your house?"

She was coming around to my way of thinking. I couldn't help but smile. "Sort of like inviting Dracula into your house."

Ito gave me a sly look.

The guard put the phone down. With a cold look on his face, he pushed a button and the gate went up.

The front door to the mansion opened as I pulled the car around. Instead of the butler and his crisp, white shirt, there stood a hulking giant of a man. Well over six feet tall, with blond, shaggy hair, a craggy face and green eyes. He looked well muscled in his black suit. As we walked closer, I could see a tattoo on his neck, mostly covered by the white shirt. He wasn't someone you brought home to your parents.

"Hey there," I said. "Aren't *you* intimidating?"

I slugged him in the shoulder and felt nothing but brick.

"Jimmy," warned Ito.

The giant lead us through the house and out into the pool area, where Robert and Eva were waiting. He sat in the shade under an umbrella, wearing sunglasses and a light blue golf shirt with khaki pants. The butler, in his crisp, white shirt, handed him a lowball glass with probably very good whiskey in it, which explained why Incredible Hulk, Junior had answered the door. The butler departed, passing us as he went back into the house.

Eva was over by the pool, wearing a white wrap with linen pants, topped off with one of those large, floppy hats. She was barefoot and held a glass of white wine in her manicured and jeweled hand.

"Good afternoon," I said, pulling off my sunglasses.

"Can I get you two anything?" asked Eva.

"We're here on an official matter," I answered using my I-mean-business-voice.

"Official? Sounds serious," Robert replied, not a little sarcastically.

Ito leaned toward me. "Take it down a notch."

"And what business do you have?" asked Robert. "Was the check not big enough?" He took a sip of whiskey.

I had no idea. I hadn't looked at the check yet. Looking from Robert to Eva and back again, I said, "I was hoping to speak with Patrick."

A moment of silence.

Robert said, "That's not possible."

"And why is that?"

"He's not here," replied Eva.

My heart skipped and started pounding. I swallowed. That wasn't right. He had to be here.

"Where is he?" Ito asked, frowning.

"He left," Eva said simply.

"As you might imagine," Robert explained, "his experience was quite traumatic. After giving his statement to the FBI, he didn't feel he could get the help he needed here in Los Angeles."

There was a buzz in the back of my head. Robert wasn't telling me the truth.

"And the FBI was OK with that?" asked Ito in disbelief.

Robert said to her, "We assured them he would be a great witness. Once they apprehend the last kidnapper."

"Where did he go?" I asked. "Because I have some questions for him."

"Under what authority?" asked Robert.

"We'd rather not say," said Eva with a sniff.

I turned on her. "You'd rather not *say*?" I couldn't believe what I was hearing.

"It's for his own protection," she said. That was the truth. "He's afraid. There is still someone out there that hurt my son." And that was a lie.

"They're hiding him," I said to Ito, then turned to the Beverlys. "You're fucking *hiding* him."

The giant stepped closer to me. In the fallout from this latest development, I'd all but forgotten he was here with us by the pool. I could hear him sucking in air through his nose. I glanced up at him.

"I'd like you to meet our new head of security," Robert said. He put his glass down with a thunk on the glass tabletop. "He's from Eastern Europe. He doesn't speak much English, but he comes highly recommended."

Ito stepped forward. "All right. OK. Enough fun and games." She glanced at the Beverlys' new head of security. "Even you know the word 'cop' so back off."

To his credit, the big guy looked at Robert, who nodded slightly, and then took a step back.

"Where is Patrick?" Ito asked again.

"Why do you need to know?" said Eva, raising her wine glass to her lips.

"Why? Because he's a witness," she replied.

"A killer," I corrected. "He's a killer."

Ito's eyes darted to me. "Not helping," she said from between her teeth.

Robert stood up. "When it's time for him to testify, of course, he'll come back to America — "

"America?" I said. "He's not even in the *country*?"

Ignoring me, Robert finished, "You have my word."

"Your *word*? Are you kidding me?" I looked at Ito in desperation. "They're covering it up! Patrick killed Matty. He killed Edward. Maybe even Benny." I looked at the new head of security. "Or were you the one who took care of that loose end?"

The big man grunted and stepped closer to me. His eyes were daggers.

"Step back," ordered Ito, as she put her hands on her hips. It didn't go unnoticed that the move emphasized her service weapon on her hip.

Big Man rocked back on his heels, crossing his arms.

"I think it's time you leave, Mr. Cooper." Robert Beverly nodded to Ito. "Detective."

"No, no. Not yet," I said. I couldn't breathe. This wasn't how it was supposed to go. It was supposed to all unravel for them. I looked at Eva. "What happened the night I found him? Did he come clean? Did he explain everything and you just had to fix it?"

Eva's voice broke. "He's my son," she said.

"Eva," Robert cautioned her.

"Please," I said. "I know you love your kid, but this isn't right. This isn't — "

But once again, Eva was as unfeeling as stone. "You've been asked to leave, Mr. Cooper," she replied. Her eyes were wet, but her face was steel.

I felt Ito's hand on my arm. It started with just a touch, but then became a pull.

"Let's go, Jimmy," she said quietly.

I didn't even feel my feet on the ground as I headed back into the house.

Robert shouted a parting threat at my back. "Keep your mouth shut, Cooper, or there'll be a defamation suit so big your grandchildren will be still be paying for it!"

Ito led the way out of the house. I didn't dare slow down. The head of security made sure to stay right on my heels, looming large behind me. Maybe if I had been a bigger man or had paid any sort of attention to Dad when he taught me some fighting moves during his action hero days, I could've taken this guy.

Spoilers: I'd still have gotten my ass kicked. The guy was huge.

The Beverlys' front door closed behind us in a very final way.

Ito was halfway to my car when I snapped. "That's it?! You're going to let them kick us out?"

She turned to me, a weary expression back in her eyes. "There's nothing I can do here, Jimmy. Unless they're going to admit anything — "

"Then let me get them to admit it!" I pleaded.

She paused and looked right at me. "They told us to leave. I have no probable cause to go back in."

"They're paying everyone off! And where they can't...!" I shook my head. It couldn't end like this. "What about Matty?"

Ito put up her hand. "All of this is built on circumstantial evidence. Without hard proof, their lawyer would — "

"You mean my mom?" I jabbed back.

She paused. "Yeah. I guess I do."

"What would she do?" I took a breath and faced facts. "She'd get any indictment tossed. The prosecutors would look like idiots."

Ito nodded. "Sounds about right."

It sounded exactly like what would happen.

"And prosecutors famously don't like looking like fools," she said.

I mustered a quiet, "Fuck." I looked up at her. "So that's it then? It's all over? They won?"

Ito looked at the house and then at me. She gave a slight shrug. "I don't know. Maybe? Money goes a long way, but it's not forever."

# 33

___

THE SUN HAD set by the time I got home from one of the worst days I had had in a very long time. It had been a very quiet drive back from the Palisades. Nothing kills a vibe like a big dose of humiliation. What was supposed to have been a great, winning moment for both of us had turned to ash. Good times.

I had dropped Ito back off at her precinct, and as she left my car, Violet turned. Hand on the open door she said, "You're going to be OK, Jimmy."

I nodded, glad it wasn't a question.

"I'll see you later," she said before closing the door and heading back into work. I watched until she disappeared through the door, wondering when later would be.

As I headed to my place, I thought about Patrick Beverly. Wherever he ended up, he was never going to be a truly free man. He was always going to be looking over his shoulder. His wealth would give him some protection, but maybe Ito was right. Maybe it wouldn't be forever. Maybe the feds would finally get him and bring him back and Matty would get some justice.

Maybe someday. But now it was really truly out of my hands.

There wasn't anyone waiting for me when I got home. Dad's luggage was gone. I stood in the middle of my living room and called his phone. It kept going to voicemail. Getting worried, I stepped outside, thinking I'd get back into my car and go searching for him. Car keys in hand, I tried to remember any of his old haunts.

Moe was stepping out his place, pulling on a T-shirt. "Hey, Jimmy. I saw that you just got home — "

I put up a hand, interrupting him. "I'd love to chat, but Dad's not answering his phone. I'm, uh, I don't know..." I didn't want to admit that I was worried about my father.

"Honey," said Moe in a way that I knew meant bad news. He swallowed. It must've been really bad if he didn't want to tell me. "He's gone."

Blood drained from my face. "What?"

"I mean — *sorry*. Oh my God." Moe blanched. "No. He's gone, not *gone* gone. He left."

I put a hand on my chest. "Jesus, Moe, I thought..." Then I realized what he had said. "He left?"

Moe nodded. "A few hours ago."

I shook my head, not quite believing it. "Where did he go?"

He looked away. "He didn't tell me. I assume back to Vegas."

"Did he say *why*?"

Moe smiled grimly. "He just waved at me as he loaded up. I tried asking, I tried to convince him to leave a note or call you, but he just kept making jokes and said he needed to beat the traffic."

Fuck.

"I'm so sorry, Jimmy."

I nodded, wishing I was still drinking at the very least. A bottle of vodka would have turned that sharp pain under my ribs into something a little duller, something a little easier to put my arms around. Or ignore. The lizard stirred. "Shush," I mumbled.

"What did you say?" Moe asked.

"Nothing."

Silence hung between us.

"You want to come in and have tea with me?" he offered. "There's cookies. Freshly baked."

I shook my head.

"Or dinner! Come on over. Watch me make dinner."

"No, it's OK."

Moe took a breath. "Are you sure? You don't have to be by yourself right now."

With a rueful smile, I said, "I've been through this before. It didn't kill me the last time."

He looked at me, then agreed, saying, "If you need me…"

I nodded and headed back inside.

The place was oppressively quiet. I ordered a pizza and threw on a movie. I needed something big and noisy. Something that would drown out the lizard. *Demolition Man* it was. I wasn't going to relapse over Paul Cooper.

I called Erika before pressing play.

"Hey," I said.

"Hey right back," she replied.

"I'm watching Sly Stallone and Wesley Snipes duke it out. You want to watch it together?"

"Jimmy, I've had a long day. I don't want to come over."

I sighed. "It's going to get longer."

"What do you mean?"

"You'll love the beginning. It's starts with me saying, 'You were right.'"

---

PART OF THE story was in the news the next morning. None of the important stuff, like Robert and Eva Beverly colluding with their son to cover his murders and help him flee the country. Rather, it was all of my mistakes front and center. The quotes from Agent Alexander were particularly damning. She suggested if I had left it to the "professionals," everything would have turned out OK. Matty would still be alive, and they would've arrested the conspirators. She ended the interview with the *Times* by saying the hunt was on for the third kidnapper and that he would soon be in custody.

Sure, Jan.

I pulled into Century City, listening to McCartney's "Let Me Roll It." The valet sourly held the door open for me and took my spot in the driver's seat without a word. It was going to be one of those days. I rode the elevator up to Cooper and Associates. It wasn't hard to believe that everyone else in the lift was pretending I didn't exist.

When L.A. turns against you, you'll know.

I passed through reception, and they barely looked up. On the way to my office, I saw Nora at her desk. When she saw me, she stood up quickly. At least she still cared.

"They didn't tell me you were here," she said by way of apology. "Normally, the valets…"

I shook my head, telling her not to worry about it. "They read the newspapers. I'm currently to blame for Matty's killer getting away."

"But that wasn't your fault, was it?"

I wondered. Was it?

"No, it wasn't," I said.

She nodded. I would explain it to her later, but at that moment, I didn't want to unpack anything about the case. "I was going to get some coffee," she said. "Would you like some?"

"Terrible coffee sounds great. Thanks."

She nodded and smiled. As she hooked a bit of hair behind her ear, she headed to the break room and I turned into my office.

Mom was there, sitting in my chair. "Good morning, James." Her tone suggested that she, of course, had read the papers.

"Morning," I grunted.

"Just so you know, the Beverlys have decided that my services are no longer required."

I slumped. Of course. "Listen, if this is going to be some sort of lecture about how I let the billionaires get away, can we skip to the end?"

"It's all right," she sighed. "They weren't going to be great clients. I suspected as much when their little monster tried to BS his way through his witness statement."

I raised an eyebrow. That was why she visited me during Patrick's interview.

"You're not the only one who can tell when someone is lying, James." She took a breath and pushed herself out of her — *my* — chair. "Erika told me about Paul slinking away."

I nodded slowly.

She moved closer. "He was always an asshole. I'm sorry you had to relearn that lesson."

"Quite the pep talk, Mom."

She patted me on the shoulder and started to leave.

"Did you know he was here all along?" I asked.

She looked at me with a knowing smile and left.

I took a breath and closed my door. I needed some time away from the looks and what I believed everyone was thinking.

But I couldn't get Paul Cooper out of my mind. He had snuck out again in the middle of the night, metaphorically speaking. The last time he did that, I wasn't in my right mind to find him, much less to get some answers.

But now... Now I was a big boy, with lots of therapy under my belt. And I knew the city he lived in. With those two facts working for me, it didn't take me long to find a phone number for Paul Cooper of Las Vegas, Nevada.

I pulled out my phone and typed the number. My thumb hovered over the green button, and then I thought better of calling from a number he would recognize. It would be easy to ghost.

Listening to the dial tone of my office phone, I went over what I was going to say and took some breaths to calm down. I didn't want to be mad. I didn't want to yell at him.

OK, that's not entirely true. I was upset, but I did want to hear from him. I wanted to know if what I thought happened between us had actually happened. I wanted to say that I would be there if he wanted to talk.

I dialed. The phone rang a few times, and finally, someone answered.

"Hello?" It was a girl's voice. Maybe ten years old.

I checked the phone's display. I had the right number.

"Yeah, hi. Um." I tried to sound upbeat, friendly, but I was confused. "I'm looking for Paul Cooper. Is he around?"

A beat. "No, Daddy's not here," she said in a singsong voice. "He's at work. You want to speak to my mom?"

No. No, I did not. I hung up just as she was calling to her mommy.

I closed my eyes and tried to breathe. The silence was deafening, and I didn't want to hear from the lizard and its ideas. I plugged my phone into my computer and scrolled anxiously for the right song.

"Santa Monica" by Everclear. That'd do it. Nice and loud. I didn't care that Mom would say "It's a workplace." If she did, I'd ignore it. Because fuck it.

Nora knocked at the door. File in hand, she said over the music someone was interested in hiring me and it sounded like an interesting case. She said they wanted Jimmy Cooper and I almost ask why. I didn't. I nodded and told her she could leave the file on my desk. I told her I'd get to it. I turned away from my desk. It didn't matter that someone wanted me. I couldn't look at it now.

I had lost the case. I had lost my dad. I stared out at the city and didn't feel a damn thing. What did it matter if I *was* Jimmy Cooper. Big fucking deal.

The lizard agreed and started coming up with some ideas. And they were all tempting.

Taking a breath, I knew what I needed to do. I reached for my phone and dialed a number. I was sweating as I listened to it ring. Finally, a familiar voice answered.

"Hey, Jimmy," said Gordon Bixby. His voice was welcoming and kind. "I was just about to call you."

The End.

# Song List

Smashing Pumpkins — Today

Kindness — Swinging' Party

Albert Hammond — It Never Rains in Southern California

Harvey Danger — Flag Pole Sitta

Prince — Pop Life

Harry Styles — Sign of the Times

The B-52s — Planet Claire

The Specials — Ghost Town

Jenny Lewis — She's Not Me

Dolly Parton — Here You Come Again

Shungudzo — It's A Good Day (to Fight the System)

The Dave Brubeck Quartet — Take Five

Tim Curry, *The Rocky Horror Picture Show* — I'm Going Home

Haim — Hold Me

Ten Years After — I'd Love To Change The World

Orchestra Baobab — Mouhamadou Bamba

Ani DiFranco — Pulse

The Only Ones — Another Girl, Another Planet

Material Issue — Valerie Loves Me

LP — The One That You Love

The Breeders — Cannonball

Paul McCartney & Wings — Let Me Roll It

Everclear — Santa Monica

The playlist can be found at...
YouTube Music: https://bit.ly/BFDYouTube
Spotify: https://spoti.fi/3PhrLEF

# Special thanks to...

FIRST, I WANT to thank everyone who had a chance to read the first book in the series, *Big Fat F@!k-up*. The response and enthusiasm made writing this second one easier.

I need to thank Enni Tuomisalo, who created another spectacular cover for me.

This book would be nothing without my editor, Jessica Hatch. She is insightful, generous with her creativity, and on top of things. She understood what I was trying to do and kept me on track when I lost my way. Thank you, Jessica.

I also want to thank some early enthusiasts and supporters: Adam Burton, Stephanie Fry, Kevin Paul, and Joanna Ryan Becker.

And, of course, I have to thank my family, who have always supported my work.

This book was written under some challenging conditions, so a thank you to my son, Joshua, for being patient while his dad got pages done. And to my wife, Deepti Gupta, you are my ally and my biggest and toughest fan. I wouldn't be able to do this without you.

And thank you for picking up *Big F@!king Deal*. If you've enjoyed it, please tell your friends!

Until next time!

— LA

Jimmy Cooper will return in

# Go F@!k Yourself

To stay up to date follow Lawrence Allan on Instagram @WriteLarryWrite or join his newsletter: LawrenceAllanWrites.substack.com
You can also find him at **LawrenceAllanWrites.com**

Made in the USA
Monee, IL
28 October 2023

45368102R00192